EL LOBO

Lobo Watkins, known as El Lobo, had been hell on earth — but, having decided to hang up his guns, he was now a prosperous rancher. What then had brought him back to Cravett? Was it Sadie, the girl he'd left behind? Whatever the reason, this impressive man was going to clean up the town and rid it once and for all of land-grabbers and those who sought to impose their rule on the community. But it would take all Lobo's prodigious skills and determination. Would he live to see it through?

0135979597

VIC J. HANSON

EL LOBO

Complete and Unabridged

LINFORD
Leicester

First hardcover edition published in
Great Britain in 2003 by
Robert Hale Limited, London
Originally published in paperback as
Guns of Lobo by Vern Hanson

First Linford Edition
published 2004
by arrangement with
Robert Hale Limited, London

British Library CIP Data

Hanson, Vic J.
    El Lobo.—Large print ed.—
    Linford western library
    1. Western stories
    2. Large type books
    I. Title
    823.9'14 [F]

    ISBN 1–84395–515–6

Published by
F. A. Thorpe (Publishing)
Anstey, Leicestershire

Set by Words & Graphics Ltd.
Anstey, Leicestershire
Printed and bound in Great Britain by
T. J. International Ltd., Padstow, Cornwall

This book is printed on acid-free paper

1

There were about three-dozen riders in the bunch and they rode hard. At their head on a huge black stallion was a big man with a leonine grey head beneath a battered Stetson. He was old and his great body was beginning to sag. But there was something terrible about the look on his heavy, lined face and he used his spurs savagely.

The black horse responded nobly but could not wholly outstrip the rawboned grey mare at its flank. This mare was ridden by a woman. She wore mannish riding-clothes; but in this country of wide-brimmed hats she was hatless and her yellow hair streamed like a banner in the wind. Hers was a comely face but her expression was hard and furious.

The riders were like avenging furies. Not even when they sighted the town shimmering in the heat-haze before them did they slow down but, if that was possible, urged their horses to even greater speed.

Out of the heat-haze three more horsemen appeared and galloped towards the wild bunch.

The two parties, the large and the small, came together in a swirl of dust. Horses, reined in suddenly, reared and snorted, tearing the ground beneath their hoofs.

The three newcomers were young and they looked scared. The voice of one of them rose shrilly above the medley of sound.

'You're too late, Mr Craddock! Too late!'

For a moment there was comparative silence. Then the silence was torn as the old man cursed, savagely, vilely.

He looked at the woman then; but he did not apologize for his language.

But it was almost as if she had not heard. She stared at the young man who had spoken and her lips mouthed words but no words came. Then the wild bunch, with the three newcomers among them continued on towards the town.

The galloping of hoofs reached a crescendo once more and the woman's eyes blazed but were tearless. Her lips still moved — almost as if she prayed — but no words were audible above the din of hammering hoofs.

The bunch stopped so suddenly again that for a moment it was completely hidden by dust. Then the dust cleared and horses and riders were held as if by a spell. And even the dumb beasts seemed to be staring in grief and rage at the cottonwoods.

'Cut him down,' cried the old man.

Then, after a time, he said, 'He'll ride with us.'

Only he, King Craddock, would have thought of such a thing. Without expression now, he watched two of his men lash the sagging body upright in the saddle of a riderless horse. The woman watched too. There was horror in her eyes but her face was frozen; all of her body seemed frozen as if she could not move, could not speak.

When the wild bunch swept down on the town King Craddock had a new companion in the saddle of the horse beside him, a companion who grinned and bobbed and wasn't at all put out when the walls of the town belched hot lead.

The woman had left the wild bunch. She had not wanted to do so but King Craddock had furiously ordered it, and the King was not a man to be gainsaid. Besides, if resistance was long she might still be of use in the enemies' camp.

The three young horsemen had left too, before the attack started. It was not their fight. They hit the trail for places unknown. They had had their bellies full of the hell-hole called Cravett.

A fancy name for a cowtown. But not a fancy place!

King Craddock and his followers met a hotter reception than they had bargained for. Evidently they had been

4

expected. King's grinning companion jerked twice as he was hit. The old man himself was almost knocked from his horse by another slug.

Bloody history was made that day. And when it was finished a broken wild bunch straggled back to its home territory with its broken leader in its midst. They left behind the one who was to have been saved.

He lay in the centre of the main drag, head lolling on broken neck, body riddled with lead, battered by the hoofs of panic-stricken horses.

There was no revelry in Cravett that night, for the town had suffered wounds and losses too. When the broken body was carried from the street and through the side door of Cravett's biggest honky-tonk by a yellow-haired woman and an oldster with a pegleg, nobody paid much heed.

Some said it was she who had fetched King and his boys. But she was a fearless well-liked woman and still something of a power in town. Didn't she own the finest honky-tonk this side of the Rio, and wasn't she the world's best when it came to picking the girls? So, they let her be. She had her grief too, for the broken body she had saved from the dogs and the elements was the body of an old friend. Some said he had been her man. Only he it seemed had been able to get past that hard shell, to bring new light to those cold eyes, animation to the beautiful, hard face.

So, only three people attended the funeral of the man who had been lynched, and she was one of them. Just three of them. Yellow-haired Sadie Cane, her old friend and general factotum Pegleg Brown, and an itinerant preacher who called himself Holmes.

No mannish riding-clothes for this trip but finery to flaunt in defiance before the town. And Preacher Holmes had more sense than to make any remark about disrespect for the dead. If it came to that, Cal Jensen would have probably wanted Sadie that way on their last trip together. He had been a

6

snappy dresser too, and a law unto himself. Until the law of the rope caught up with him. Preacher Holmes had his own views about the justice of hemp-law in this particular case but he saved his breath to intone his sermons, which was all anybody would allow him to do nowadays.

The following night Cravett was outwardly back to normal. Sadie's establishment was open again. She moved among her guests and answered greetings and her eyes seemed no more watchful than was usual.

Guards had been placed around the town in case of another attack. But only one rider turned up, and he brought the news that King Craddock was dead.

An era was ended. As the news was passed from mouth to mouth in Sadie's place talk died slowly, music ceased. All eyes turned toward the tall man in black broadcloth who sat at a poker-table with three of his cronies.

Duke Roland rose to the occasion — and to his feet. He was an imposing figure. He lifted one large immaculate hand and cried:

'The King is dead! Long live the King . . . Drinks are on me!'

If some people wondered where Duke had picked up the fancy quotation they did not waste time in speculating about it but joined the general rush for the bar. It didn't do to speculate overly about Duke anyway. He was what you might call an educated killer: twice as deadly as the ordinary wild type.

Sadie Cane mounted the ornate staircase to her room. She was busy bathing her sore feet when there was a knock on the door. She called 'Come in' and Duke entered.

'Get out of here,' she said from between tight lips.

He smiled thinly, the smile not reaching his eyes. 'What's got into you, Sadie? We agreed we'd always be friends.'

'Friends!' She spat out the word. 'Get out, I said!'

'Surely you don't blame me for what happened.'

'Blame you? Yes, I blame you. You could have stopped it. Only you could have stopped it. But you let it happen. Did you think that with Cal out of the way I'd . . . ' Words seemed to fail her but her eyes mirrored hate and contempt.

'Nobody talks to me like that,' said Duke Roland.

She laughed harshly. 'So now the King is dead, the Duke would be a King.'

Passion inflamed his usually sallow features. He seemed as if he would spring on her. But he spun on his heel and was soon gone, the door slamming behind him.

The woman's face crumpled but she fought herself. If a side-winder like Roland could be a King, well then, she would be a Queen. But a Queen in opposition to the King, a Queen who would some day have the King's head.

★ ★ ★

The marshal of Cravett was Mike Daventry. He had once been a noted fighting man but was now old and broken-down and addicted to periodic bouts of rum-swilling. He was a mere token lawman, tolerated and supplied with booze as long as he behaved himself and turned a blind eye to the depradations of the town hardcases.

Cravett was a long way from a Ranger headquarters or soldier camp. It was a 'wide-open' town. It was near the border, conveniently so for any man with a price on his head. Lawmen and bounty-hunters visiting the place were met by a sullen boozy marshal and a bunch of townspeople who didn't seem to care a rap for law and order.

No young man would take on Mike Daventry's job. Mike had been enrolled by Jake Priest, mayor of Cravett. But Jake was long dead and there was now no mayor. Old Mike even found difficulty in getting deputies, except for such official mockeries as hazing drunks or dog-catching.

After the Battle of Cravett, Mike made bloodcurdling threats of sending for the military and having the place razed to the ground. But an increase in income suddenly came his way and he went on a blinder. There was no other visit from Craddock's Triangle C boys. Their numbers were sadly depleted and, above all, they had lost their leader.

So for a couple of weeks after the battle things were unusually quiet in town. There wasn't a single gunfight and no gougings or kickings of note. Then a rumour started to get around that a relative of Cal Jensen was here to avenge that hellion's death.

Sadie Cane was the first to meet the newcomer. One night Pegleg Brown knocked on her door, put his head around it and said, 'Sadie, there's a Mr Jensen here to see yuh.'

Sadie's hand flew to her breast. Then she cursed herself for her silly fancies and said, 'Send him in.'

Hat in hand he stood blinking under

the bright lights after the semi-darkness of the passage outside.

Was this man really a relative of lusty raven-haired Cal Jensen? Was this the man who had come to avenge Cal's death?

He turned his hat slowly round and round in his big-knuckled red hands. He was tow-haired and pale-eyed and his mouth hung open a little, though that might have been because he was temporarily bulldogged by the magnificence of his surroundings and the flamboyant beauty of the woman who confronted him.

She was like something out of a picture-book and he had just come in off the trail and his faded clothes hung on his lean frame and he stank of sweat and horseflesh.

'Please sit down, Mr Jensen,' said Sadie. 'I was just making coffee. Would you like some?'

He found his voice. 'Yeh, sure, ma'am — that's mighty nice o' yuh.'

The hot coffee seemed to loosen his

tongue. He lost his sheepish look too.

'I came looking for Cal,' he said. 'I just heard what happened to him. A character downstairs said you might be able to tell me more about it.'

'What was Cal to you?' she asked.

'He was my brother.'

2

Clay Bogaine was Cravett's bully-boy. Every cowtown had one. Fast with fists and gun. Not over-bright. A show-off and a bragger. Quick to take offence, particularly if the cards were stacked in the right direction. Proud of the notches on a greased and well-worn gun.

Clay Bogaine carried two guns. He might have been boss of Cravett, if Duke Roland hadn't turned up. Duke was cleverer and faster. He was quiet and cold like a side-winder. He only rattled before he struck. Clay was a little in awe of him. Duke listened to Clay's bragging and praised him and made him an ally when another less smart man might have made him an enemy.

Clay Bogaine heard of the man who had come to avenge Cal Jensen's death.

The stranger's name was Bruno Jensen and he claimed to be Cal's brother, though they must have been as unlike as any brothers could be. Bruno, there was a name for you, guffawed Clay Bogaine. If the yellow-coloured cissy started ructions in Cravett, he, Clay, would personally take care of him and save that drunken old coyote, Mike Daventry the job.

Clay and the dead Cal Jensen had been at logger-heads for some time before the latter's shameful death. There had been much speculation as to who might be the victor if things finally came to a head between the two men. Maybe, now Cal was dead, and the bully-boy had had more than a hand in that too, Clay Bogaine hoped to vent his spleen on the so-called brother too.

He didn't have long to wait for the chance to do so.

A couple of nights after the first one in which Bruno Jensen was seen, the word got around that the newcomer was out looking for Cravett's bully-boy.

And leaning on the bar in Sadie's place Clay Bogaine bragged and waited.

He knew it as soon as Bruno entered the place, although he didn't spot him right away.

A hush spread over the place — slowly. Talk died. Laughter and music died. Then there was only the rather stealthy scraping of feet as people fanned away on each side of the place, hugged the walls and the staircases. The gap widened until there was nothing between Clay Bogaine and the door, except a few small chairs and tables — and the man who called himself Bruno Jensen.

Bruno moved forward haltingly. His gait was clumsy and he didn't look at all dangerous. Some people thought he looked a little scared — like a tenderfoot aiming to have a go at something he knew he couldn't possibly accomplish.

When he was halfway between Clay and the door he stopped. When he spoke his voice was halting too. He said:

'You led the people who killed my brother.'

'How come?' said Clay, savouring the moment. He acted as if he had all the time in the world.

'You led the mob.'

'Somebody had to be in front of them. But they knew what they aimed to do all right.'

'I'm calling you out.'

'Are you now?' jeered Clay. He was no taller than Bruno — they were both tall men — but he was broader. There was a dark hairy brutish look about him; his teeth were a little prominent and they gleamed wolfishly like fangs when he grinned.

He was grinning now as he said, 'Cal Jensen was a skunk anyway. He only got what was coming to him.'

'I'm going to kill you, Bogaine,' said Bruno Jensen.

'What are we waiting for then?' said Clay still grinning. His one elbow was on the bartop and his thumbs were hooked in his belt.

17

He straightened up and moved a little way away from the bar and took his hands away from his belt. Then he crouched a little, elbows bent, hands poised a little way above his gun, fingers clawed. It was the traditional gunfighters' stance, a little florid, a stance not adopted by every gunman. But Bogaine knew how to play to the grandstand.

He took a long single step forward. He brought his other foot forward, slowly levelling. His knees were bent a little as he braced himself.

Bruno Jensen did not move. He held his arms straight at his sides, his hands a little way away from hips. He only wore one gun, in a shapeless floppy holster, which wasn't tied to his thigh by a whangstring, the way both of Bogaine's holsters were. Bruno didn't look like a gunfighter; he looked like a simple cowhand who was forcing himself to do what he had to do. His gun had the cheapest scarred walnut butt. There were no notches on it the way there were notches on the butts of

Bogaine's twin pearl-handled Colts.

Bruno's face was grey and set. His eyes seemed to have a puzzled look as he stared at Bogaine and waited. The seconds ticked away.

Bogaine's eyes were hooded now beneath heavy brows. A good gunfighter always watched the other man's eyes. Sometimes the other man's eyes gave him away with an infinitesimal flicker before he went for his gun. But you couldn't see Bogaine's eyes, only the taunting leer on his heavy face, you only knew that Bogaine's eyes were the flat pale eyes of the born killer and even if you could see them they wouldn't give anything away.

And now Bogaine had savoured the moment to the full and was all through waiting.

'What're yuh waiting for, yeller-belly?' he said. 'Draw!'

Bogaine was not very original with his taunts. Bruno Jensen didn't seem to hear them anyway. He made a few steps forward. Shuffling almost. Then he went for his gun.

Only one shot sounded. Both Bogaine's guns were out. Blue smoke wreathed his hips. Bruno Jensen's gun was only half out of its holster when the first slug hit him. He flopped over sideways as if somebody had kicked him treacherously. But Bogaine's second bullet missed him and he straightened up and got his gun out. He was moving forward again as he fired. His bullet smashed a bottle on a shelf behind the bar and he kept moving — hoppity-skip — as if, not hitting his enemy he meant to grab him and crush him with bare hands.

Then Bogaine's second shot hit him, knocking him back, spinning him half-around. Bogaine was grinning. His eyes were wide-open now too, and they were pure evil.

Somebody gasped. A woman gave a little horrified yelp, like a stifled scream. Bruno had lost his bit of headway but he was trying to make it up again. Bright droplets of blood shone on the floorboards in front of him but he was still miraculously on his feet, he was straightening himself up, still clutching his gun, raising it.

He was signing his own death-warrent. Bogaine was all through playing around. He was no longer grinning. As he raised both his guns, his eyes were pale, strange, cruel.

Another shot sounded. But Bogaine's guns did not jerk, no flame and smoke issued from their muzzles.

Bogaine was slammed back against the bar. He dropped one gun and cursed vilely as he clutched at his shoulder with the free hand. His eyes rolled, glared upwards as he tried to lift the other gun.

'Drop it, Clay!'

It was a woman's voice. All heads were swivelled as people realized that the last shot had not come, miraculously, from Bruno Jensen, but from above and behind him.

Bogaine let his second gun join its fellow on the boards at his feet. Sadie Cane came slowly down the stairs, a

Colt in each hand. A thin thread of smoke still drifted from the muzzle of one of them.

Another woman screamed as Bruno Jensen fell flat on his face in the centre of the floor.

Pegleg Brown came forward, another man at his heels. Between them they picked Bruno up.

'Take him upstairs,' said Sadie. 'Put him in my spare room.'

Clay Bogaine continued to prop the bar up, his face going greyer and greyer.

'Fetch the doc, somebody,' said Sadie.

'Somebody already done gone,' she was told.

Blood seeped through Clay Bogaine's fingers where he clutched his shoulder. He stared at Sadie with pure hate in his eyes. But she still held her guns kind of steady, she didn't miss a trick. 'Give him a drink,' she said.

The barman pushed a man-sized tot of whiskey across to Bogaine. The gunman knocked it back, shuddered.

The little cortége of Pegleg and his companion and their limp burden turned the bend at the top of the stairs and was lost from view.

'I guess he ain't got a Chinaman's chance,' said an oldster, shaking his head regretfully. 'He's buzzard-bait right now. But he certainly had guts.'

'Fetch the sheriff, somebody,' said Sadie Cane.

Little Doc Masters came bustling in. Behind him was Preacher Holmes and the youth who had gone for the doc. Seemed like the boy had already explained what had taken place. The doc crossed to Bogaine, scrutinized him sharply, then called:

'Somebody get bandages an' fix this wound. It's just a clean hole. He'll keep for a while.'

He whipped around at Sadie. 'Where's the other one?'

'Upstairs. In my spare room,' she rapped.

Then, as the doctor bustled up the stairs, Sheriff Mike Daventry entered the place.

He looked about him with bleary eyes. 'What's going on?' he demanded truculently.

'Arrest this man, Sheriff,' said Sadie. She pointed at the glowering Bogaine. 'He just shot a man. The man may be dead.'

'It was self-defence,' said Bogaine. He looked about him as if waiting for somebody to back him up.

Maybe somebody would've done — he had plenty of friends among the tough element — had not Sadie been there, her guts still very much in evidence too.

But now the oldster who had admired Bruno Jensen's guts spoke up. 'The younker never had a chance.'

Then Sadie's voice rang out again. She knew how to play to the gallery too. Compared to her Bogaine was just an amateur. 'Do your duty, Sheriff,' she cried.

Old Mike Daventry looked about him as if seeking some means of escape. Then he looked at Bogaine and took a few shuffling steps forward.

'Get away from me, you old buzzard,' snarled Bogaine. 'Or, by Gar, I'll have your scalp.'

Mike halted fearfully. He wasn't quite sober. He blinked his little red eyes. The gunman was like a cornered rat. Wounded, but still able to strike.

'Do I have to do your job for you, Sheriff,' said Sadie Cane.

Her voice dripped with contempt. It seemed to lash Mike, bring him some sudden awareness of himself and what he had become. He straightened his bent shoulders a little. He stole a half-shamed glance at Sadie, who still held her two guns. He looked again at Bogaine and Bogaine's two guns lying at his feet.

The sheriff took out his own gun. 'I gotta take you in, Clay,' he said.

The gunman shrugged evilly and gave in. As the sheriff shepherded him to the door, he was promising the gunman that he would fix that shoulder.

Preacher Holmes appeared at the top of the stairs and called Sadie. An ominous sign. The preacher's face was set in a lugubrious mask. A ripple ran through the room. Sadie hurried forward.

* * *

For three days Bruno Jensen lingered on the brink of death. He had a bullet in his shoulder and another one in his chest. The latter had nicked his lung and that was the worst thing of all.

The first bullet had gone through the fleshy part of his shoulder, clean through and out the other side. This was, in fact, an even cleaner wound than the one Sadie had given to Clay Bogaine.

But the second bullet had buried itself deep and lodged, and little Doc Masters had to operate to get it out. The cantankerous little man had been an army surgeon during the Civil War and was used to emergencies. Sadie acted as nurse and anaesthetist during the ticklish job and Pegleg Brown, Sadie's 'extra arm', did the fetching and carrying and afterwards the doctor praised them both wholeheartedly. They had proved a fine team, the bluff little doctor, the saloon queen and the grizzled one-legged mossyhorn. Strangely enough, Cravett respected all three of them. And there was no denying that between them they saved Bruno Jensen's life.

The doc did the spadework and the other two finished the job off. The hard-boiled Sadie proved a real angel of mercy, staying by Bruno's bed and ministering to his wants both night and day. She wasn't seen downstairs again until Bruno began to turn the corner.

For those first three days he was barely conscious most of the time and he babbled in delirium. He repeated a girl's name over and over. *Lucinda*. He mentioned another name too. Yes, it was so obviously a name, though many a listener might not have thought so. A strange name. A nickname rather. *Lobo*.

He mentioned his brother's name too, but not so much as the other two. It was as if even in his delirium he realized that his brother would never be with him any more.

Sadie was folding his clothes, preparing to send them to be cleaned of bloodspots when she found the letter, the address. She put the letter in her desk, meaning to replace it when the togs were returned from Ling's Chinee Laundry.

When Doc Masters called on the evening of the third day the patient was beginning to look around him and recognize people.

Sadie was overjoyed. She had taken a shine to this saddle-tramp the way she would've to a wounded and endearing pup. But the doc cautioned her not to be over-optimistic.

'The young man's pretty stringy and tough,' he pronounced. 'But I have known cases like this to take a turn for

the worst. Even now he could go off
— like that!' He snapped his fingers
briskly.

It was then that Sadie decided to
send a message to the person at the
address she had seen on the letter.

3

Pretty soon the rainy season started in; and with it came another stranger.

Lopez of the livery stable was the first to see him and, strangely enough, to Lopez he was no stranger. Lopez moved a little way from his door, ignoring the rain which quickly soaked him to the skin.

'El Lobo.' Lopez half-whispered the name. No man who had fought in the Border Legion could possibly forget El Lobo, the Wolf. He was hunched a little in his voluminous slicker, bent a little against the wind and the rain. In such a way Lopez had seen him once before and now he was reminded of those times. The fighting, the horror, the comradeship. And the romance too, of those times. Aa-iii.

He ran into the storm, waving.

'Señor Watkins!' The wind took the

30

words and tossed them carelessly away. But the horseman had seen him and was gentling his mount to a stop. The figure had straightened and was staring towards Lopez in the twilight and through the slashing rain. Lopez went nearer and called again. The rider turned his horse's head then and urged him slowly nearer and Lopez knew the hand would now be on the gun — perhaps it was already pointed from beneath the shelter of the slicker.

'Señor Watkins,' Lopez called again. 'Captain.' He knew that Lobo no longer used that title. But it worked, the rider recognized him, called his name in return. And next moment the livery-man had hold of the horse's bridle and was leading it into the livery-stable.

He closed the doors behind them, shutting out the noise of the storm. Lobo Watkins divested himself of his dripping slicker and sat himself before the fire in the little lean-to which adjoined the stables.

Lopez seated himself opposite and

handed across a mug of hot black coffee. They did not say much, these two men, they did not bombard each other with questions. They sat looking at each other and grinning a little, sharing memories. It was almost as if the years had never parted them. It was Lobo who, rising, asked the first question.

'*Amigo* — where can I find a woman called Sadie Cane?'

Lopez told him. He also promised to look after his old friend's horse.

He added then, 'If at any time you need me, you can always find me either here or at the cantina next-door-but-one. My friends and I are always at your service, *el patrio*.'

Lobo bowed gravely, said thank you, and left.

Night had fallen now, a night of black lowering skies, the rain needle-sharp with the wind. Lobo followed Lopez's directions. He would not have had any difficulty in finding Sadie's place anyway: he was not the only traveller seeking its warmth and conviviality: its bright lights beckoned from afar.

Lobo had slung his slicker across his shoulders as he braved the storm and now as he opened the batwings he shook it away from him and the sawdust was spattered with bright drops. It was early yet and the place was only half-full. Heads turned automatically, eyes surveyed the stranger. But Cravett was used to saddle-tramps and this one didn't seem at all out of the ordinary. Nevertheless, it wasn't wise to stare too long at anybody in this lawless South-West, and the heads swivelled back to their gaming, their drinking, their ogling of percentage-girls.

Lobo Watkins was a medium-sized man of around thirty. His face was lean, his mouth mobile; there was a deceptively drowsy look about his eyes. He dragged his slicker on the floor as he made his way to the bar. He was evidently a person who didn't set great store by such mundane things as clothes. His high-heeled riding boots were badly scuffed-over. He wore tattered and mudstained chaps and an equally beat-up leather vest with sheepskin lining. His check shirt was of an unidentifiable well-washed colour and his kerchief was a mere rag. Unruly brown hair escaped in wet tendrils from beneath his sopping battered Stetson.

He bellied up to the bar and leaned on it with his right hand hooked in his gunbelt. This was well-worn too but good — and loaded. The gun was a Colt .45 with a smooth walnut handle. The holster was tooled leather, obviously of Spanish origin. It was tied to the thigh by a whang-string: some people might have thought that a particularly significant fact.

Lobo's wet slicker was now in a heap on the brass rail at his feet; he called for a rye. The barman served him with studied indifference but his profession had taught him to read men and he weighed this one up. Not looking for trouble, but well able to handle it if it came.

The man knocked back his drink and took another, holding it as he half-turned to survey the room. Sadie Cane was coming down the stairs and their eyes met. She gave an almost imperceptible jerk of her head, then turned and retraced her steps.

The stranger finished his drink, placed the glass carefully on the bartop and meandered away. The barman watched him meander up the stairs. The barman's speculative look would probably have changed to one of surprise had he seen them meet on the shadowed landing and kiss before walking on to the room at the end.

Bruno Jensen almost shot out of bed. 'Lobo! By all that's holy, what brings you here?'

Sadie took it upon herself to answer this question. 'I sent for him,' she said. 'I found his address in your pocket when your clothes went to the laundry. I knew he must be a great friend of yours because you spoke his name a few times when you were delirious. You see, a few days ago, the doc thought you might die. You fooled him — he says now he thinks you must be made of teak . . . '

Bruno opened his mouth to say something but shut it again. Sadie went on: 'Besides,' she drawled, 'I ain't seen my old friend, Lobo, in years. I didn't even know whether he was alive or dead. I guess this was the best chance I'd ever have to make him come a-running.' She gave Lobo a mischievous sidelong glance. 'He never did that before.'

For a moment Bruno thought she looked like a young girl with her first crush. He held out his hand and his friend gripped it. 'I'm mighty glad to see you, Lobo, even though I ain't dying.'

'I got news for yuh, pardner,' drawled Lobo.

'What's that?'

'Lucinda will arrive here on tomorrow's stage. I guess she aimed to see you before you died too.'

'For Pete's sake — a convention!' said Bruno. But he could not disguise his gladness at the news.

There were footsteps in the passage, then the door was flung open and Doc Masters bustled in.

'What's this? Too many visitors — no good — too much excitement. Patient's not out of the wood yet, you know.'

The little man was introduced to Lobo and then Lobo and Sadie took their leave. Over a piping hot supper in Sadie's private sitting-room, the dance-hall queen told the story of how Bruno got shot.

Lobo waited until she had concluded, then he asked, 'And is this Clay Bogaine still in jail?'

'No, the sheriff had to let him go. He had nothing to hold him on. It was self-defence. Bruno went for his gun first . . . '

'Yeh, I guess he aimed to avenge his brother. The damn fool, he should've known he was no match for a slick gunnie. So, the case is, to all intents an' purposes, all finished up, huh — the sheriff's finished with it.'

'The sheriff's a drunken old coot,' said Sadie. 'The thing would've been finished right at the start had he had his way. I had to bulldoze him to make him lock Clay Bogaine up. The way Clay calmly shot Bruno to pieces made me see red. I should've killed Clay while I had the chance — he'd certainly be no loss to the community. All I did was give him a gammy shoulder, and that's getting better fast by all accounts.'

Lobo had no comment to make on this. 'Who is sheriff of this burg?' he asked.

'A broken down mossy-horn called Mike Daventry. He was once quite a hellion I'm told — but that must've been before my time. If this town had some good law enforcement it might amount to something.' Sadie's voice was bitter.

'Wait a minute,' said Lobo. 'Did you say Mike Daventry just then?'

'I did. Why — do you know him?'

'I used to,' Lobo was thoughtful. 'Yeh, Mike certainly must've changed.'

It was Sadie's turn to ask a question. 'What brought Bruno here in the first place. Did his brother Cal send for him or something?'

'No, I don't think they ever corresponded. They hadn't seen anything of each other in recent years. I never met Cal myself — only heard Bruno talk of him. It's like this.' Lobo leaned forward, continued:

'I own a little spread. The address you sent your letter to: that's my place . . . '

'Lobo, you a rancher!'

'Yeh, why not? I guess I've done enough hell-raising to last me for the rest of my life. I figured I'd settle down for a while.'

'I notice you said for a while.'

Lobo grinned, let it pass. 'Bruno ramrods the spread for me . . . ' He paused, grinning at Sadie's raised eyebrows.

'You don't think Bruno looks the

ramrod type huh? Believe me, Bruno's one of the finest cowmen I've ever met and for all his mild looks he's got authority, too. I send him on buying trips sometimes. That's what brought him out here. He had to go to a place about ten miles away. He told me he'd call on his brother while he was nearby. It must've been a great shock to him when he learned what had happened, no wonder he went off half-cocked.'

'He certainly did, tangling with a hardcase like Clay Bogaine.'

'Bruno never was great shakes with a gun,' said Lobo sadly. He paused, his eyes narrowing.

After a moment he said: 'You never actually told me why the mob got Cal Jensen.'

So Sadie told him the whole story, trying to keep her voice as unemotional as possible. It was easier to tell it to Lobo than it would have to anybody else. She tried not to relive it too deeply, for it was a harrowing story.

There had been a gambler in Cravett

called Jasper Coutts. He was a friend of Duke Roland (Sadie explained who Duke was), though they weren't partners or anything like that. On the night it all happened Jasper had been bucking the tiger at one of the faro layouts downstairs. The dealer at this particular table was a little half-crippled hardcase known at Limpy Rome. He had ridden into town about two months before and asked Sadie for a job. She had given him a trial and found him to be one of the best dealers she'd ever come across. She didn't know much about him, except that he came from Texas. It wasn't part of her policy to ask her employees personal questions. As long as they did their work well and behaved themselves that was good enough for her, and Limpy proved to be a gem — though he kept himself very much to himself.

Probably Limpy's only real friend, strangely enough, was Clay Bogaine. Sadie wondered whether the two men had known each other before, but she hadn't been able to find out whether this was a fact or not. That night had been a quiet one, the tables were not overly patronized, and Jasper Coutts had challenged Limpy Rome to a game of stud poker and into this Cal Jensen and another man, who takes little part in the story, had joined.

Things came to a head pretty quickly. Then it all happened in a few seconds and two men lay dead. Cal accused Jasper of cheating and Jasper went for his gun. Cal shot Jasper and, as Limpy moved, shot him too. He said Limpy had also reached for a gun.

Cal was going back to King Craddock's spread where he worked, when the mob caught him.

'It was self-defence wasn't it?' said Lobo Watkins.

'Yes,' said Sadie. She paused.

Then she said: 'I didn't see it. I only heard about it, heard the mob. When I got down there it was too late.'

She went on to tell Lobo of how she had ridden to the Craddock place. She had had a faint hope that 'the King' might be able to save his boy. She told of the battle and King Craddock's subsequent death.

'What inflamed the mob so quickly?' asked Lobo.

'Some people said that although Jasper Coutts had been killed in self-defence, Limpy hadn't gone for the gun the way Cal said he had. I know that Limpy always carried a Derringer in the waistband of his trousers. Cal was hotblooded and reckless but he wasn't the sort to shoot down a man in cold blood for no reason at all. I guess nobody really saw what happened. Limpy was Clay Bogaine's friend and Cal was his enemy. Clay led the mob.'

'What's this Clay Bogaine do for a living?' asked Lobo.

'Who knows?' said Sadie. 'Who knows what most of the hardcases in this town do for a living? They ride out bunches from time to time, sometimes with Clay at their head, others with Duke, sometimes with both of them and the whole goshdarn bunch.'

It seemed like Lobo had at last finished asking questions. Sadie could think of nothing more to tell him. She felt exhausted, dried-up.

Outside the saloon Lobo asked a lounger the way to the sheriff's office. He found Mike Daventry drowsily playing Patience with a half bottle of whiskey at his elbow. He peered blearily at his visitor.

'Hello, Mike,' said Lobo softly and clearly.

Mike rose slowly to his feet. His eyes focused, recognition slowly dawned in them. And something else too. What was it: shame, fear, or the awakening of something more admirable?

'Lobo,' he croaked. 'Lobo Watkins!'

'How are you Mike?' Lobo stepped forward and took the old man's hand. He noticed that Mike had to hold on to the desk with the other one and he felt a flash of pity.

But the old mossy-horn had never needed pity before.

'I guess all you need, old-timer is a new deputy,' said Lobo softly.

4

Pegleg Brown told the barman that night of the identity of the new stranger. The barman, whose policy it was to be friendly with everybody, passed on the news to Clay Bogaine.

'Lobo Watkins,' said Clay. 'He's got quite a rep hasn't he? He used to be a ball of fire with the Border Legion I'm told. What's he doing in Cravett?'

The barman grinned. 'He came to visit a sick friend — Bruno Jensen.' He left Bogaine to digest this titbit of information.

Bogaine took it with him over to a table where Duke Roland was in session and after a time was able to get Duke alone and pass on the titbit to him.

'Well, what are you worried about?' said Duke laconically. 'I don't expect the fabulous Lobo will pick a fight with a man with his arm in a sling.'

'Hell, I ain't worried,' burst out the one-armed Clay. 'I ain't scared of Lobo Watkins — even if he is hell on wheels. I'm just wondering whether visiting a sick friend is his only reason for coming to Cravett.'

'I guess we'll find out about that later,' said Duke. 'Anyway, one man, even if he was the best shot in Kingdom Come won't make much difference to us. What's more important is for you to get that arm well as quickly as possible. I've got a big job in mind, the biggest ever.'

'What's that?' whispered Bogaine hoarsely.

Duke told his henchman to keep his lips buttoned and then, dropping his voice to a conspiratorial murmur too, gave him the gist of the proposed job.

Bogaine's little eyes got a little wider. Then he breathed finally, 'By Gar, if we could pull *that* one off!'

But Duke was looking past his

companion now and Bogaine turned his head and he, too, saw the sheriff enter with his new friend.

Mike Daventry was steadier, sprucer and more erect than he had looked for a long time. His new found air of authority was more than matched by the demeanour of his companion who had a bright new deputy's star pinned to his vest.

Quite a few people in Cravett had food for thought and dreams that night. Clay Bogaine, with a gammy flipper and a feeling of uncertainty; Duke Roland, a little mystified; Sadie Cane, happier than she had felt she should be after the loss of a dear friend; Mike Daventry, with the awakening of a new life in his whole body; Bruno Jensen, with a happiness that more than matched Sadie's and, despite his ills, a dream of the morrow like a kid's on Xmas Eve . . .

And Bruno's dream came true.

She stepped off the stage in the sunshine to the delight and edification of the more somnolent of the population. But they kept their mouths shut when they saw that the new deputy was waiting to escort her. The word had got around about Lobo Watkins and it needed little embellishment, for there were very few people who had not heard of him and his exploits at some time or other.

She was small and dark, a modish prairie flower complete with portmanteau and hatbox. Lobo had carried these into the saloon and Sadie came forward. The two women greeted each other without affectation, the gold and the dark; it was as if they liked each other on sight.

'Lucinda is the daughter of my oldest hand back at the ranch,' explained Lobo. 'He's acting as foreman while Bruno and I ain't around. He's a real bobcat too, only I don't like the old coot to work too hard.'

Lucinda gave a little ripple of laughter. 'You know Dad, Lobo,' she said. 'He'll probably have the whole ranch painted inside and out by the time you get back.'

'And all the cattle too I shouldn't wonder,' grinned Lobo.

Sadie led the way upstairs. The trio paused finally outside Bruno's door.

'I'll get something fixed up to eat,' said Sadie and elbowed Lobo in the ribs with a force that made him gasp. But he took the hint and followed her along the passage. Glancing back, he saw Lucinda enter the room, he heard her glad cry of greeting. Lobo figured Bruno would be sitting up in bed grinning all over his face. His recovery from his wounds had been little short of miraculous. Lobo was glad Lucinda had come, glad he had been able to give her good news as soon as she stepped from the stage, glad that Bruno was backing him up so wholeheartedly. But things were far from right in Cravett and he hoped Lucinda wouldn't stay too long.

Sadie was bustling around in the kitchen. Lobo took a seat. Sadie flung words over her shoulder.

'So now you're a deputy sheriff. Whose idea was that?'

'Mine own, *chiquita*.'

'What about your ranch?'

'That'll be all right. Old Buck Sanders — that's Lucinda's father — is a real humdinger. I couldn't have left the place in better hands. Anyway, there ain't any big doings there at the moment.'

'Somehow I can't see you as a rancher,' said Sadie.

'Why not? I never aimed to be a troubleshooter all my life.'

'Why the star now then?'

'Women!' snorted Lobo. 'The questions they ask a man! Well, I'll tell yuh. Mike Daventry is a very old friend of mine, though I ain't seen him in years. He wasn't always a drunken old wreck. He saved my life once . . . '

Lobo paused, made a little inarticulate gesture with his hand. Then he burst out again, 'What Mike is going through now is a kind of death I guess.

Maybe I'll be able to save *his* life now.' He went on in a rush of words: 'Besides, I aim to stay with Bruno till he's better an' we can go back home together.'

'If I remember rightly,' said Sadie, 'you were wearing a star the very last time I saw you.' She made a clatter with pots and pans. 'That's why I guess whenever I've thought of you it's been as a fighting man rather than a rancher.'

Lobo rose, skirted the table and went over to her. She had her back to him. She had had her back to him all the time. He put his hands gently on her shoulders.

'How long ago was that, huh? Two years — three years?'

'Can't you remember?' she said softly.

'Yeh, I remember.'

'Three and a half years,' she said and turned towards him.

They kissed and then, like a shy girl with her first beau, she turned once more to her tasks. Then, as Lobo

51

perched himself on the edge of the table she said:

'You sent me away then 'cause you had a job to do and a woman had no part in it.'

'When the job was finished I tried to trace you,' said Lobo. 'But I couldn't.'

'And you never expected to find me here, proprietress of a hell spot?'

She turned towards him again and he grinned at her. 'Yours is a great and honourable profession, *chiquita*. Women like you have helped to mould the West. An' I ain't just being pompous when I say that. I guess I misjudged that prairie flower those years ago when I sent her away. She was the kind who'd stand by a man in any kind of trouble.'

'She should have stayed,' said Sadie. 'No matter what you said then, she should have stayed. She went too easily.'

She elbowed Lobo out of the way and began to lay the table. Then, after a time — and apropros of nothing — she said, 'You figure you've got a job to do here too, don't you, Lobo?'

'I guess so. If I don't do it that young fool along the passage will try to as soon as he's fit.'

'And it's no good my telling *you* to leave this time.'

'No.'

'Well, you've bitten yourself off a sizeable chore. But I guess I'll be allowed to help this time, huh?'

They faced each other, looking at each other. Lucinda came into the room. 'He's going to be all right, isn't he?' she cried. 'He's going to be all right.'

* * *

There was much speculation in Cravett about the new deputy. People couldn't remember old Mike Daventry ever having a deputy before. Even if he had, they probably hadn't stuck the job long. Some people wondered at the old buzzard having the nerve to hire a man. But this deputy was kind of different and maybe with him at his back Mike Daventry figured he could cock a snook at his erstwhile 'friends'.

Lobo Watkins had been out of the news for quite some time now as the years wrote their lawless pages in the history of the great South-West. But his legend still lingered and the stories were recounted now. How he had cleaned up this town, how he had cleaned up that one. His was a history that, despite the fact that he was still a young man, was almost as fabulous as that of Wyatt Earp, Bill Hickok, Bat Masterson and Ben Thompson.

But the fabulous Watkins let off no fireworks that first day. He was seen around town both alone and in the company of the sheriff. And he was very affable towards the townspeople, very gentlemanly towards their womenfolk, until some people began to say that this Watkins had been very much overrated, or that this man wasn't the notorious Lobo at all but somebody using his name.

Sheriff Daventry was cold-sober and almost soldierly in his bearing. He looked ten years younger. How to explain this transformation?'

Then, on the second day, Mad Jake Morgan chose the time to make one of his periodical sorties on the town.

Mad Jake was a prospector, or at least that's what he claimed to be. His face and head were covered with a tangled mat of red hair and he was always filthy. Naturally, he looked older than he really was, but when roused was hell unlimited. He was big and lean and hard and for a weapon favoured a sawn-off belly-gun rather than a pistol. In the hands of an expert like Jake this piece of hardware was a terrifying thing.

Mad Jake brought his horse and burroes into town about noon and stashed them at the Lopez stables. Then he made tracks for Sadie's place and draped himself across the bar. He paused once for a meal but by nightfall was well and truly lit-up. Then the rafters rang as he threw back his shaggy head and let loose his war cry, like the howling of a demented timber-wolf. This was the signal that Mad Jake Morgan was about to take over the town, and men, women and children should run for cover.

Strangely enough, Jake never seemed to do much damage in Sadie's place. He liked Sadie; she had once doctored him when he limped into town with a terrible abscess on his leg. Seemed like even in his craziest moments Jake didn't forget this Samaritan act. Most people treated him like a mad dog. Maybe that was why he acted like a mad dog. Or was it the other way around?

The terrifying war cry was the signal for people to fan out and clear a path between Jake and the batwings. He watched this manoeuvre going on with his head on one side and every appearance of vindictive satisfaction. A beanpole character with a vivid red check shirt was a mite slow and Jake hurled a bottle of whiskey at him. The puncher ducked, dived into the crowd like a startled hare. The bottle exploded on the batwings, leaving them swinging crazily. The smell of rotgut hooch smote the air with raw violence. A startled face appeared above the top of the batwings, legs jittered below them. Then face and legs disappeared as if whisked away by a magician's hand.

The barman moved a little and Jake turned on him. 'Back!' he roared. 'Back, you knock-kneed skunk.'

The barman retreated nervously and got ready to take wings. Sadie Cane began to come down the stairs. Jake saw her and rolled his head and winked and grinned in what might have been a salutation. Then he started his weaving bull-like approach to the batwings. A chair got in his way and he kicked it aside. A table too, was tossed into the crowd. The ordinary townsfolk peered and backed and tried to efface themselves. The hardcases, to whom Jake was a necessary evil and perhaps a source of enjoyment too, looked up from their gaming and wenching and grinned.

Somebody yelled: 'Mad Jake the talking b'ar!'

Jake stopped, tree-like legs spread apart, and looked about him as if seeking the would-be comedian. His eyes sparkled, they were brighter than his red hair, they glowed like coals deep in a thicket. Jake showed his teeth in a fearsome grimace.

There was a scurry of movement from the onlookers as he spun suddenly on his heels and tacked his way back to the bar, from which he grabbed a full bottle of whiskey.

Sadie was at the foot of the stairs now. 'You, Jake!' she yelled. The giant pulled the cork with his teeth, spat it out on the boards. He tilted the bottle to his lips, threw back his head and took a deep swig. Then he started to march again.

'You'll pay for that booze, you big ape,' yelled Sadie.

Jake turned his head, wagged it, grinned like a gargoyle. He waved the bottle over his head. Some of the whiskey gushed from the unstoppered mouth, anointing Jake's unwashed mat. 'I love yuh!' he boomed. It was hard to say whether he meant the bottle or the girl. He continued onwards.

He didn't walk lopsided because he was drunk. Liquor seemed to have more effect on his brains than on his legs. He walked lopsided because he had his favourite belly-gun down the leg of his pants. He reached the doors like a cutter in the wind.

Sadie wasn't scared of Mad Jake Morgan. Maybe she understood him too well. Maybe she knew that no matter how drunk he was he wouldn't harm her. Her progress was impeded by men of little courage. Nevertheless, she managed to call the giant a few choice names before Jake passed through the batwings into the darkness. His gargantuan laughter floated in the air behind him.

The assemblage breathed a collective sigh of relief. But a few seconds later nerves were frayed once more by the tremendous blast of a shot from the night. A man ran in and said Mad Jake had blown the windows out of a cantina down the street.

The sounds of his progress were wafted back on the breeze from time to time. He always went by stages, stopping now and then for more liquor or to grab food and hastily wolf it. Sometimes misguided citizens got in his way; foolish types had been known to try and reason with him.

The story of this particular night's progress was to be told over and over again and embellished in the process. As usual, Jake made a full circle. Strangely enough, Jake always returned to Sadie's place. He had even been known to sleep there. Quite probably he paid Sadie for liquor he had stolen and damage he had caused, though such was not the case in other establishments he visited.

He broke all the windows in Papa Pablo's cantina and stunned two fractious greasers by the simple expedient of knocking their heads together.

He called in at Frisco Kate's cathouse and his booming laughter shook the gaudy frame building as he chased the girls and tossed a few assorted visiting firemen through convenient apertures.

Halfway round the circle he visited the livery stables once more, only to be met by Lopez with a sawn-off shotgun twice as big as his visitor's. Jake boomed that all he wanted to do was say 'Howdy' to his hoss and his burroes. This he was allowed to do (it was even said later that the delighted Lopez supplied him with a fresh bottle of whiskey) and he told his four-footed friends what a hell of a time he was having before, roaring with laughter, he went once more on his way.

He broke into a bath-house and ducked the attendant in one of his own tubs, insisting on soaping the terrified fully-clothed man all over before completing the process.

From time to time he paused to reload his shotgun, only to discharge it almost immediately. It was a mercy he didn't kill anybody. He burst into a gaming house and wrapped a roulette wheel round a fancy gambler's neck. He shot out the lights in a dance-hall. He pulled up a hitching-rail by the roots and filled the main drag with loose cayuses. His war-cry filled the night like the wailing of a demented banshee; his laughter boomed as loud as his shotgun.

He kept on drinking but he didn't seem to get any more drunk; he just got wilder as he approached the end of his usual circuit. He deviated from time to time, that was the most terrifying thing about him — nobody knew where he might strike next and barred doors and windows seemed of little avail — but he always finished up back at Sadie's.

And this time, when he got back there, Deputy-sheriff Lobo Watkins awaited him.

Lobo had been out riding. Jake was

well on his round when Lobo returned to town. Mike Daventry was sitting in the sheriff's office smoking. There wasn't a bottle in sight and Mike was as sober as a judge. He explained that, not wishing to have a hole as big as his head blown right through him, he always let Jake wear himself out.

The old man grinned sardonically. 'I ain't aiming to stick my neck out for this town,' he said.

Lobo said, without a trace of pomposity, 'We've gotta have complete law enforcement here or none at all.'

Mike rose. 'All right,' he said mildly. 'Let you an' me take a leetle pasear.'

Mad Jake's progress was bewildering. Despite the noise he made, he covered his tracks with animal cunning. There were intervals of silence too, before his war cry, his laughter or his gun broke forth again in a direction from whence you least expected it. It was the sheriff who, having more knowledge of their quarry's ways than his companion,

63

suggested they beat Jake to Sadie's place.

So it was that the old lawman ranged himself beside his deputy at Sadie's bar and, with just a small tot to keep him company, waited.

The night was now long in the tooth. There was a lull in sound and only the soughing of the night winds. Everybody waited. There was the click of poker chips, the clink of glasses, the swish of cards, but very little conversation; only small sounds which seemed part of the general stillness, the waiting.

Duke Roland held court over a stud-poker game and was his usual arrogant and imperturbable self. At his side Clay Bogaine, arm in sling, tried to emulate his boss. But he couldn't seem to keep his eyes off the sheriff's companion. Was this the fabulous El Lobo? He didn't look any great shakes. And what did the fabulous Lobo aim to do now: take the tiger by the tail an' twist it?

The comparative silence was suddenly broken by a crash from outside as of a house falling over. Then heavy foot steps thudded on the boardwalk. Mad Jake Morgan had come to the end of his round trip and he sounded kind of tired. Here at the end of his journey it was a tradition to let him be. He would be through with his hell-raising and was all right if you let him be. But he was pretty mean when he was tired — he didn't laugh any more — and it wasn't wise even to speak to him.

The batwings swung open with a crash and he lurched into the saloon, blinking his eyes against the light and looking more huge and red and fearsome and filthy than ever. He held his wicked short-barrel shotgun at waist level, the muzzle pointing forward.

He was halfway down the lane that had been made for him before he spotted the two men in the cleared space at the bar. He faltered a little in his teetering stride. Then he shoved the muzzle of the gun forward a little, his fearsome head with it, and continued onwards.

The two men at the bar fanned out a little. Then the younger one started to walk forward, his hands swinging loosely at his side.

Jake stopped dead, legs spread wide. Nobody had ever approached him like this before at the end of one of his sorties.

He screwed his face up in one of his special and most awful grimaces. 'Keep still, you dancing puppy,' he boomed. 'Or I'll cut yuh plumb through the middle.'

Lobo Watkins drawled, 'A night in the hoosegow will do you a power of good, Jake. You better give me your gun. I'll take care of it for you.'

Jake put his head on one side as if he couldn't believe his ears. Otherwise he didn't move. His belly-gun was as steady as a rock and aimed dead centre on Lobo Watkins. Lobo kept on walking.

Somewhere a woman gave a little

sob. People waited for Lobo to be blown to Kingdom Come, a crazy finish to a legend.

Then Jake did a surprising thing. He let his shotgun fall at his feet. He strode over it. He rushed. He flung his arms round Lobo Watkins.

A woman screamed shrilly now. A man shouted, 'He's gonna crush him to death.'

But people who stood nearer to the two men striving in the middle of the floor were staring as if they couldn't believe their eyes. The giant was kneading the other man's shoulders. 'Lobo,' he was muttering brokenly. 'Lobo.'

And Mad Jake Morgan was crying like a child.

5

The next couple of days saw a transformation in Mad Jake Morgan. Although he didn't actually turn into a tenderfoot, he was hardly worthy of the sobriquet of Mad Jake any longer. Outwardly, anyway.

He had his hair and beard trimmed and bought himself some new togs, including a huge cream-white Stetson which made him look like a fugitive from a three-ring circus.

His beard, clean and glossy now, was redder than ever. He looked like a clown. But it was significant to note that he still walked with his lopsided stride.

He still drank, probably more copiously than most men. But he might have been imbibing milk for all the effect the stuff had on his temper. He even spoke softly to barmen, and at least twice he was caught in the act of raising his hat to a lady.

He took a room at Sadie's place and bright and early every morning sauntered resplendent down the staircase to join his two pards, Lobo and Mike at their breakfast. The only thing he didn't do was sport a shiny tin star.

Days stretched into weeks and Jake showed no signs of setting off on another of his expeditions. Things in and around Cravett were pretty quiet. From time to time cowboys from the Craddock ranch were seen. But there were no hostilities.

Clay Bogaine had his arm out of the sling and swung it at his side, though it still seemed a mite stiff. Lucinda Sanders stayed on, helping to nurse Bruno who continued to improve rapidly. Ex-drunkard Sheriff Daventry and ex-wildman Jake Morgan seemed to be trying to outdo each other in their new roles of reformed characters. Deputy Watkins was affable to everyone, though taciturn; he always seemed to be around someplace.

On one of his periodic rides Lobo Watkins made a call on the Craddock ranch and met the taciturn grey-faced woman who called herself Mrs Craddock. She gave him the traditional welcome a big old-fashioned ranch of this kind would give any traveller. But she would talk only commonplaces. The punchers he met were just as unproductive. Lobo had heard from Mike the story of the Battle of Cravett. He wondered if the Craddock faction were planning revenge. One could hardly blame them if they were. If they did attack the town again, Lobo rather wondered where he would elect to stand. The way he saw things, sixty per cent of the townsfolk were ripe hangman's bait. But, after all, he was a lawman now, pledged to protect the town from lawlessness. Riding back from the ranch he unpinned the star from his breast. He almost threw it in a mesquite patch. But with a wry grin he replaced it. At least it was a means to an end, although he wasn't quite sure yet what that end would be.

The Craddock spread was now ramrodded by a man called George Pinfold. Lobo had heard of Pinfold who, by all accounts was youngish and pretty capable all round, but he had never met the man or even seen him, which seemed rather strange. Lobo wondered whether for some reason Pinfold was deliberately keeping out of his way or whether Pinfold was just around the ranch at the present time but out on a trip somewhere. There had seemed to him to be a sort of atmosphere of waiting about the ranch. Was everybody waiting for the return of Pinfold?

But the plans, if any, of the Craddock faction were suddenly curtailed in a very dramatic fashion a couple of nights after Lobo's visit.

★ ★ ★

For three days there was a lull in the rain and a watery sunshine bathed the plains. Then at noon on the fourth day the heavens opened again. By nightfall the wind was at gale force, driving the rain before it in icy pellets. Thunder grumbled and the clouds were torn apart by lightning.

Sadie's place was open later than usual and in the warmth and smoke and conviviality did a roaring trade. When it finally closed people gushed through the doors, scattering in all directions, running for cover across the black treacled mud.

In a short time the main drag was empty. Pegleg Brown put the shutters up on the windows of the saloon, drew the double doors and vanished inside. Lights went out one by one. Cravett was given over to the blackness, lit fitfully from time to time by jagged lightning, to the wind and the driving rain. A lean cur dog streaked across the main drag and found shelter the other side. It wasn't even fit for him to be out.

An hour passed. A cat emulated the dog. Cravett slept. Timber groaned, resisting the fury of the gale. Somewhere a loose board flapped from time to time, making a sound almost like a pistol shot. And along the backs of the buildings men and horses began to appear. They all met, about two dozen of them, a little way out of town.

'Is everybody here?' said Duke Roland.

'I guess so,' said Clay Bogaine. 'I'll make sure.' He kneed his horse forward, weaved in and out of the other riders. He spoke names gruffly, received soft replies.

Somebody else counted in a dull monotone. Men were spacing themselves out now, calling to each other, comparing notes. The wind carried their voices away.

Duke Roland said, 'Not so much noise. The wind might carry it back to town.'

Clay Bogaine rejoined him and said,

'Everybody's here.' Duke's burly *segunda* had both hands on the reins. His gammy arm was better.

'Let's go,' said Duke and led the way — away from town out on to the range where the wind whipped at horses and men, the rain stung them, the lightning bathed the cavalcade from time to time in ghostly white light.

'By Gar, what a night to be out,' grumbled one man, huddled shivering in his slicker.

Clay Bogaine heard him, turned on him. 'It's the best night we could've picked. Leave it to Duke, he knows what he's doing.'

Duke set his horse at a gallop. The others streamed after him. They began to descend the slope of a shallow valley and Duke halted them finally in a patch of scrub and stunted cottonwoods which partially sheltered them.

'Stay put,' he said. 'Clay and I are going down to reconnoitre.'

A few seconds later the blackness swallowed the two men up. But they soon returned and Duke began to give out with the orders.

The bunch were split into two sections, Duke leading one and Clay the other. They would take the herd on both flanks. Clay and Duke reckoned there were only about four night-riders and they would hardly expect trouble on a night like this. Clay and his bunch started out first because they had to make a detour.

The others waited, bent against the storm, taking care to keep their weapons dry beneath their slickers.

'Get ready,' said Duke.

The men pulled their kerchiefs up over their mouths and noses, made sure their hat brims shadowed their eyes. Huddled like spooks in voluminous slickers or blanketcoats, there was little danger that any of them would be recognized. Duke snarled at a man whose kerchief was white, prominent in the blackness. The culprit took it off, stuffed it away out of sight, replaced it by a dark kerchief he borrowed from another man.

The first shots sounded from down below. Duke waved his arm, spurred his horse forward, led the headlong charge down the slope.

The night-riders on this flank were streaking to the help of their comrades round the other side of the herd. They were taken completely by surprise, engulfed by the second wave of attackers. Very little extra shooting was needed. The two men were left where they had fallen. The cattle were skittish from the storm. The shooting completed their demoralization. In a sluggish black mass, they began to move. But they gathered speed quickly and the riders had to set their mounts at a gallop to keep up with them.

The steers had their heads, nobody tried to guide them, for this was not necessary. Pretty soon they ran themselves out, slowed to a walking pace. Duke joined Bogaine in the van to compare notes.

'I guess they're going roughly in the right direction, huh?' said Bogaine.

'Yeh. Did you fix the riders your side?'

'Yes, we fixed them all right.'

'So I don't expect we'll have any trouble from the ranch.'

'Naw. We're miles away from it now anyway.' A flash of lightning lit Bogaine's snaggle-toothed grin. 'An' heading straight for the border.'

But they were destined never to reach the border that night. Something really inconceivable happened. In that range immensity lashed by wind and rain the border-bound herd ran head-on into another herd of beef coming from the other direction, into another bunch of riders.

At this time Duke was still in the rear with his *segunda*. Neither of them knew about the new arrivals until the shooting started.

Without their leader to lend them moral courage as well as give them orders, the rustlers were thoroughly demoralized by this sudden invasion of men and beasts from the blackness. As Duke and Bogaine reached them they were beginning to turn tail. Already one of their number lay dead on the ground. A slug whipped at Duke's hat. The two leaders could do nothing else than emulate their craven followers. They could not help but be bewildered too, not knowing where these other steers and horsemen had sprung from or who they were. Duke, beside himself with rage at this rich prize being whisked so easily away from him, flung wild shots. But he kept on going, he certainly didn't want to be recognized. He hoped none of his men had been recognized either. They had all taken off their masks and would not have had time to put them on again when this bunch jumped them. Who in hell were these people anyway?

He did not learn until later that the bunch, imported gunnies, had been led by the Craddock foreman, George

Pinfold, who had picked up a fresh herd of beef on his travels too.

★ ★ ★

Bruno Jensen was mending rapidly. The doc now allowed him out of bed, first in a chair, then stepping tentatively around the room. The doc said he wasn't yet fit enough to negotiate the stairs. But Bruno it seemed had plenty of patience. Uncomplaining, he did as he was told.

Lobo Watkins had tried to persuade Lucinda to go back to the ranch, but she said she didn't aim to leave until Bruno did.

So that was that. Lobo was uneasy, he felt as if he was sitting on top of a powder keg which was due to blow at any time; he felt it in his bones.

One particular sunny morning he went to pay his usual after-breakfast call on Bruno. He opened the door, then stopped dead. Bruno hadn't heard him coming. Lobo wished he hadn't been so pre-occupied, had remembered his manners and knocked before entering. Bruno was up and he was fully dressed even to his gunbelt. He was standing in front of the dressing-table mirror practising his draw. Lobo retreated, closed the door softly behind him.

He went downstairs and had a couple of quick drinks. Bruno didn't appear on the landing as Lobo had feared he might. Evidently Bruno intended to keep obeying Doc Masters's orders. But he was trying to get his gun-hand back into shape, and Lobo didn't figure he would want to do that unless he aimed to use that hand when he finally came downstairs. Lobo became more worried than ever. Bruno would never be a gunfighter; wouldn't the crazy fool realize that until the split second before somebody plugged him clean between the eyes?

Lobo walked out into the morning sunshine, made tracks back to the office to talk things over with Mike Daventry.

Mike was his old self again, his judgement was valuable.

Come to think of it, Lobo pondered, he hadn't yet seen Mad Jake Morgan this morning. The red-bearded giant hadn't put in an appearance at the breakfast table as he usually did. Maybe he had got himself an oversize skinful last night and was still sleeping it off.

Lobo reached the office, opened the door, walked in. A stranger stood before Mike Daventry and spouted and gestured a mile a minute.

That was how the deputy sheriff of Cravett came to meet George Pinfold, ramrod of the Craddock ranch. George was a tall thin hard-bitten character with the disposition of a buzz-saw. Working for King Craddock all those years he'd just had to be that way, he wouldn't have lasted otherwise. Right now he was popping fit to bust his breeches. But there was grief in his face too. Lobo took a liking to the man.

George told a harrowing tale of four night-riders brutally murdered, of cattle stolen, only regained by a crazy fluke. Only one of the raiders had been caught and he was dead when they reached him. A hardcase who hung around Cravett, a man who would sell his gun to the highest bidder. George suspected almost everybody in this hellhole of a town but he couldn't put his finger on anything concrete.

'We found nothing else,' he said. 'No clue. Nothing. We didn't get a look at any of the skunks — you know what kind of a night it was last night.'

'We'll ride out with you,' said Sheriff Daventry and he and Lobo got their horses.

After the wet fury of the night before the range looked newly washed. The sun was gentle, for it was yet early; birds sang high in the sky.

But at the Craddock ranch, where Preacher Holmes had arrived even before the law, there were only four mounds beyond the corral around where men stood with dark vengeful faces.

'The skunks were spawned in Cravett sure enough,' said one man loudly. 'We ought to go and raze the goddamned place to the ground.'

The two lawmen wisely made no comment on this. They asked questions. Lobo saw that the cowboys mistrusted Mike Daventry. But they answered the deputy's questions civilly enough. Lobo's reputation had gone before him. He learned nothing more, however, than George had already told them.

After Preacher Holmes had finished intoning the burial service, the foreman led the two law-officers once more out on to the range. He took them to the place where he thought the night-riders must've been jumped. There was nothing there but churned turf and beaten mud drying out in the sunshine. They followed the trail of the stampede to where the herd had met the second bunch. They found nothing there either, except the expected signs of turmoil.

The two lawmen decided to try their luck back in town. They parted from George Pinfold. As the two of them rode, Mike Daventry said suddenly, 'Seemed a lot of new faces around the Craddock spread this morning.'

'Not having visited the place before I wouldn't know,' said Lobo, 'but I did notice one face I knew, that of a well-known Pecos gunslinger called Amos Moon.'

'Never heard of him,' said Mike. 'Nobody of that name worked at the Craddock place before, unless it was under an alias of course. It's more than likely he's one of the new fish I mentioned though. What's he look like?'

'Pretty easy to place. Big galoot. One shoulder much lower than the other. Long scar on his face that makes him look as if he's laughin' at some private joke all the time.'

'Yeh, I know,' said Mike. 'That's one of 'em I spotted. Looks to me as if Pinfold's importing himself some gunnies . . . Not that you can blame him after all that's happened I guess,' he added glumly.

'You've got your suspicions of the townsfolk too then I guess,' said Lobo.

'I have. So many of them that I don't know where to start.'

Mike knew he should have started years ago. Maybe his task would have been easier then, even without Lobo. Either that, he figured, or he would've been pushing up the daisies long since. But probably he would've been more proud of himself — if the dead can be proud — than he was right now.

The rest of the journey passed in silence. Lobo was doing some thinking too. He figured that the rejuvenated Mike had told him all he could think of. Probably Mike's erstwhile 'friends' had made sure their drunkard sheriff didn't learn anything that could be used against them.

Not until they were riding along the main drag of Cravett did Lobo open his mouth. Then he asked, 'Have you seen that big red skunk, Jake, this morning?'

'Not hide nor hair of him,' said the sheriff. 'Maybe he's lit out again.'

On enquiry the barman at Sadie's place said that Jake had come downstairs looking a little sorry for himself just after Lobo had left the place. Jake hadn't stopped for breakfast or even a drink, but had gone out and had not yet returned. One or two other people had seen Jake in the street, but after that it was if the ground had swallowed him. Lopez, at the livery-stable, said the red-bearded giant hadn't yet been in to wish his beasts good morning as he usually did: an eccentric and lovable habit of the big man's.

'He's probably down at the little creek ducking his head or something,' said Mike Daventry. He seemed a little peeved and surprised at Lobo's anxiety for Mad Jake.

They went on to the office to mull things over there. There seemed little they could do until nightfall and the joints started to jump. Then they would be able to mix with the tough element of Cravett and perhaps pick up a few hints about the Craddock raid.

Presently Lopez rushed in on them. Mad Jake had been found. In an alley with a knife in his back. Doc Masters was with him now.

'Is he dead?' asked the sheriff.

'Eef he isn't he's very close to it,' retorted Lopez and led the way.

The sun had gone in and dark clouds drifted across the sky. As the three men hurried along the street the rain began again and in a few seconds was torrential. They ran for cover.

In breathless sentences Lopez told his story. The little Mexican boy who did chores for Lopez had found Mad Jake huddled in the alley beside the livery-stable. There was a knife between his shoulder blades. The boy screamed for his boss. Lopez joined him. Between them they managed to get Mad Jake on to the couch in the cubbyhole in the back of the stable. Jake was still alive, but only just.

The three men entered the livery-stable which, because of the storm, was almost in darkness. They made their way to the back, passed the wide-eyed Mexican boy and joined Doc Masters. The little man straightened up, turned towards them, shook his head slowly from side to side. In a white handkerchief he held the knife which he had taken from Mad Jake's back.

'His heart's still beating faintly,' he said. 'I've done all I can for a bit. He shouldn't be moved . . . '

'He must stay there, of course,' said Lopez.

The Doc thrust the blood-stained knife forward. 'Has anybody seen this before?'

None of the three men had. The Mexican boy was called in. He had gotten over his fright now. He hadn't seen the knife before either. It was a heavy bowie with a hammered leather handle and brass trimmings. A good knife but common. Ironmongers and weapon shops in most Western town-ships carried them. They were copies made in their thousands by a firm back East.

'We'll take it, Doc,' said Sheriff Daventry. 'There might be a chance to trace the owner.'

'You might as well have the handker-chief as well.' Doc Masters wrapped the weapon up and handed it over.

The sheriff tucked the white bundle into the top of his pants and fastened his vest across to hide it. Lobo had gone past the doctor and was standing looking down at the recumbent figure on the couch. Jake looked as if he was dead. Lobo turned away. There was a look on his face that made Mike Daventry shiver, though both he and Lopez had seen it there before.

But Lobo's voice was gentle when he took the Mexican boy by the shoulder and said, 'Come and show us where you found Jake, son.'

The boy led the way. Lobo and the sheriff followed. The rain beat down at them with mocking fury. The alley was already like a quagmire and, as they had half expected, they found nothing, not even footprints.

Near where Jake was found was an old rusted plowshare covered by a tattered tarpaulin sheet. Evidently somebody had intended to pick the thing up, back in some dim time, but had either been prevented from doing so or forgotten all about it.

'I guess the skunk hid behind here and jumped on Jake,' said Lobo. 'A powerful arm drove that knife in — but I guess whoever did it figured that was the only way to fix a man like Jake an' that time o' the morning a shot would've been too risky.'

6

Jake rallied but remained in a half-coma for a long time. Lucinda and Sadie, who couldn't do much more for Bruno, took over Jake's nursing. Jake babbled in delirium just the same as Bruno had, but most of the red-bearded giant's babblings consisted of cuss-words. Lucinda and Sadie, both staunch frontiers-women, paid them no mind.

Lobo Watkins spent hours, both night and day, with his old friend. But as yet Jake could not answer any of Lobo's questions. Things came to a sudden head, however, when Lucinda was doing a spell of night-duty at the sick man's bedside.

Jake still lay on the couch in the cubby of the livery stables. Doc Masters hadn't thought it wise to move him, even to more comfortable quarters at Sadie's place.

Lopez was staying with a friend down the street and, on that particular night his little Mexican sidekick stayed in the stable to keep Lucinda company. He lay on a bale of hay in a dark corner and whittled on a stick. The boy was always whittling. He could whittle with his hands behind his back.

He was aware of the man entering the stable and at first took it to be Lobo. Then the man paused by the door of the cubby and there was a stealthy look about him. He opened the door slowly, softly, and the boy saw the glint of steel. Then, even as the gun spoke, the boy was diving from the hay.

Like a little tiger, screaming and clawing, he landed on the man's back, driving him forward into the door so that the door shut again. The man cursed vilely and shook the boy off, slashed out with the gun. The boy caught the blow on the side of the head and went down. The man ran. The boy, coloured lights exploding inside his head, yelled like mad to put them out.

The door of the cubby opened then and the lights were all one. Lucinda Sanders stood there, her face chalk-white.

When the sheriff and his deputy reached there, however, she was composed again, bending over her patient.

'The slugs didn't hit him,' she said. 'They just woke him up. He babbled a bit then dozed off again. I think he'll be all right but I've sent for the doctor just in case. Look!' She pointed.

Two slugs had buried themselves in the log wall above Jake's shaggy red head. Lobo dug them out with his jack knife. 'Colt forty-five,' he said. 'That tells us a helluva lot doesn't it? Somebody sure wants to shut this big galoot's mouth for good. Another few inches lower and they would've succeeded this time too.'

'Jake always has been a dark horse,' said the sheriff, with no hint of levity in his tone.

Lucinda told her story in a flat unemotional voice. She had been sitting on the chair beside the bunk in the darkness. Jake seemed to sleep better in the darkness. A faint light came through the small high window. Lucinda had probably been dozing a little.

'I didn't hear a thing,' she said. 'But something seemed to warn me. I started — turned my head. The door was open and somebody was there. Then the gun went off and I heard the bullets strike. Then the door slammed. It slammed because the boy tackled the killer, but I didn't know that till afterwards. I guess the boy saved Jake's life, and maybe mine too. I guess the killer meant to empty his gun and make sure. I thought he *had* made sure, until Jake woke up and started to babble. Thank God the boy's all right too.'

As if at a signal the boy entered now, and with him was Doc Masters, only half-dressed. His hair stuck up on his head like a turkey-cock.

He examined Jake. 'He'll be all right,' he pronounced. 'Sleeping like a baby. Come out of there, some of you, or you'll wake him up again.'

The sheriff and the boy followed the doctor out but Lobo lingered. 'Did he say anything important, Lucinda? Being woken up suddenly like that I thought he might've, yuh know.'

Lucinda smiled. 'Nothing but the usual cuss-words.'

'Ain't that typical!'

'Mind you, he did, I think, mention your name once or twice,' added Lucinda. 'I guess he was probably cussing you for something too, do you think?'

'Could be,' said Lobo. He realized Lucinda was feeling the strain of the sudden shock she had received, but, like the plucky miss she was, was joking to hide it. He decided he'd fetch Sadie to take over.

But he didn't need to, for just then Sadie arrived.

'Heard the ruckus,' she explained briskly. 'Half the goshdarned population is hanging about outside.'

Lobo went outside and helped the sheriff to disperse the mob. The would-be killer was probably among them, Lobo reflected sardonically wondering whether he had done his job properly or not. With that Lobo had a brainwave and put it to the sheriff. The sheriff agreed it might accomplish something and, at least, could do no harm.

So, next morning the word went around town that Mad Jake was dead, brutally murdered while he slept. The only people who had knowledge to the contrary were the two lawmen, the doctor, Lucinda, Sadie, Lopez and Lopez's diminutive side-kick. None of these would talk.

The law hadn't got a line on the owner of the Bowie knife used on Jake in the first place. Had the second attempt been made by the same man? And, thinking he had succeeded this time, would he in some way give himself away?

But nothing happened until suddenly in delirium Jake spoke a name again. And this time it wasn't 'Lobo'.

It was 'Bogaine'.

And Lobo decided on a bold move.

Mike wanted to side him, but Lobo talked him out of it. This was something Lobo had to do alone.

*   *   *

Clay Bogaine's wound had healed perfectly. His arm was as good as it had ever been. He had practised his two-gun draw over and over. He hadn't slowed down none. He was game for anybody, even Lobo Watkins, Maybe Lobo was kind of over-rated.

The sod-cutter who had had the nerve to stand up against Clay was still upstairs, though people said he was mending quickly. Clay didn't expect any more trouble with him however. Clay had gotten over his chagrin at the failure of the Craddock raid: it had been worth something to see Duke Roland's poise shattered, When Clay did a job it stayed done, he prided himself on that. All was well with the world again, he was fit to take all comers, and he wasn't short of dinero either.

He had even partially forgiven Sadie for shooting him. At least, he continued to use her place — though that was maybe only because her place was by far the finest in Cravett.

Lobo found him in Sadie's place that night. Pretty early. Not too many people in there. Bogaine stood at the bar. Lobo walked straight towards him, stopping a few feet away from him.

'I've been looking for you, Bogaine,' Lobo said.

Bogaine gave out with his usual half-grin half-leer. 'Have a drink, Mr Watkins,' he said.

'I wasn't looking for you 'cos I wanted a drink.'

'Why were you looking for me then?'

'I've got to take you in.'

'Take me in?' Bogaine's thick black eyebrows rose. 'What for?'

'On suspicion of having something to do with the killing of Jake Morgan.'

Bogaine laughed harshly. 'You can't pin that on me, friend.'

'I aim to try.' Lobo took a couple more steps forward.

'Hold it!' Bogaine's voice was thick now. 'By Gar, you ain't gettin' away with that.' He came away from the bar. His arms fell lax at his sides, then began to bend a little.

'I'll take your guns, Bogaine.' Lobo smiled thinly. 'I aim to take you in alive.' He took another couple of steps. People made stealthy movements out of the line of fire.

Lobo held out both his hands, palms upward. 'Give me the guns.'

Bogaine could have drawn then. He had the edge. But there was something about the nonchalant coolness of this man that maddened him and he knew that if he meant to win this he must be cool too.

'Get back,' he said hoarsely. 'Or, by Gar . . . '

Lobo's right hand suddenly continued its upward movement. It changed into a fist which exploded on Bogaine's chin with a dull smack. Bogaine was taken completely by surprise. He crashed back against the bar, his hands flying upwards as he strove to regain his equilibrium. Lobo gave him the left in the midriff, doubling him up. Then Lobo moved in and seemed to be wrestling with his opponent.

But when he moved away again he had Bogaine's gunbelt in his hand.

Pegleg Brown was conveniently near, grinning all over his bewhiskered old visage. Lobo handed the gunbelt to Pegleg. Then Lobo took off his own gunbelt and handed that over too.

He turned to meet Bogaine's charge, which carried him halfway across the room, skittling chairs. Both men landed in a tangled heap beneath a table.

The table went over with a crash, one of its legs splitting clean off. The two men rolled clear. Bogaine was up first. Lobo rose to one knee. Bogaine aimed a kick at him. Lobo grabbed the swinging leg, hung on to it. Bogaine managed to thrust his opponent away from him, then fell flat on his back. Both men were down then, split apart. They rose more slowly, measuring each other.

But Bogaine couldn't wait. His face plastered with blood from bursted lips, he looked fearsome as he charged. There were blue flames in Lobo's eyes. He met the charge head-on, using his fists, his elbows, even his head. Like his opponent, he had learned his rough-housing in a hard school. A roar rose from the crowd. This was a blood battle.

Bogaine had the advantage in weight. He was a cruel, dirty fighter. But Lobo was faster. He threw Bogaine away from him now with a kind of back-handed blow across the side of the neck. A table prevented Bogaine from going down completely. Cursing and choking, he grabbed a bottle from the table and flung it at Lobo's head. Lobo ducked. The bottle sailed over him, almost brained the barman and smashed a mirror behind the bar. Lobo went on, only to meet the heel of Bogaine's boot which sent him back-peddling again.

Now it was Lobo's turn to choke and grab wind and Bogaine was coming right after him. Lobo slung a chair in the big man's path. Bogaine went head-first over it and as he was falling Lobo hit him in the face with both bunched fists.

Bogaine took a couple of the members of the audience down with him this time. In their eagerness for blood they had gotten a little too near. Lobo, his face demoniacal, dived after his man and for a moment there was nothing but a glorious tangle of arms and legs.

The two non-combatants finally managed to withdraw, though not without a few minor cuts and bruises. And after that things weren't funny any more. They were kind of terrible.

Sadie Cane stood on the balcony and looked down on the scene. Her face was white, her eyes enormous. Pegleg Brown joined her. He had the two gunbelts looped over his arm.

Sadie said in a strange voice, 'Lobo's certainly chosen himself a grizzly this time. I ought to stop it,' she half-sobbed.

'I'll never speak to you again if you do,' said Pegleg. 'Don't worry, Lobo can handle it.'

Sadie winced, half turned away as Lobo went down from another sledge-hammer blow. But he was quickly up again, though he weaved a little, drunkenly.

Bogaine was in no better shape.

The fight had started suddenly, terribly. Both men had been fully dressed except for their gunbelts. Now their hats rolled on the floor in the dust beneath the feet of the crowd. The word had got around. Faces peered through the windows of the saloon, craned over the batwings.

The two men wore shirts and pants and riding-boots, kerchiefs and the usual leather vests. Lobo's vest was split down the back and gaped. A terrible grasp had done that to the tough leather. One of Lobo's shirt-sleeves was torn in strips and there was a long gash on the arm. Blood dripped from Lobo's fingertips. His face was comparatively unmarked, though one of his eyes was half-closed where Bogaine's thumb had gouged it. Bogaine's face was like red-raw beef. His leather vest was still intact, though minus both of its buttons, but the front of his shirt was torn wide open, revealing the matted black hair, blood-speckled, on his chest.

Both men were rubbery around the legs but still had power in their bodies and arms, savage destructive power.

Lobo went down again. Bogaine jumped at him, feet foremost. Had he landed where he intended to the fight would have been over right then. But Lobo rolled desperately and Bogaine came down on the boards with a crash. Lobo jumped him from behind, wrapped his arm round the bull-like neck, crooked his elbow. Bogaine's face began to go purple. He used his feet and elbows in an attempt to break the killing grip. Then suddenly he fell to his knees and arched his back. Lobo went flying over his head and landed in a sitting position against the bar. As he levered himself upwards, Bogaine threw a chair at him. It caught Lobo a glancing blow and Bogaine followed it up. Lobo braced himself against the bar and put out his foot. Bogaine ran into it and went back as if he was shot from a gun. He was almost at the batwings before a chair stopped his headlong flight. Lobo followed him. Almost on all fours, Bogaine started a bear-like flanking movement. Lobo swivelled on his heels and went to meet him. Furniture went over. People scattered in all directions.

The crowd roared encouragement, then there was a comparative hush as the two men met again and only the thud of blows, the sound of laboured breathing. Up on the balcony Sadie

Cane said, 'I can't stand this any longer,' and began to descend the stairs.

'What can you do?' said Pegleg, following her. He took one of Clay Bogaine's guns out of its holster. 'Wait,' he said.

His voice rose to a shout. 'Look, Lobo's got him! By Jupiter, he's got him!' Then a window crashed outwards as Bogaine went through it.

People scattered from flying glass and the hurtling body. Bogaine rolled across the boardwalk and came to rest finally, lying still with his head hanging over the edge.

Lobo staggered out through the batwings. He found a reserve of strength from somewhere. He grabbed the unconscious man by the scruff of the neck and dragged him along the street. He snarled at people who came forward to help him, so that they sheered away as if from a mad dog. He got Bogaine to the jail all by himself, though he was almost on his knees when he reached there. He fell into the office when Mike Daventry, who had been having a quiet snooze through it all, opened the door. Mike had been told to stay put. Now he looked mighty relieved: he shouldn't have worried, he might have known Lobo would pull it off.

Mike became very wide awake, for now he had two unconscious men on his hands, one of whom looked as if he might almost be dead.

7

'No wonder you thought he was dead,' said Doc Masters. 'When he fell on the sidewalk he broke his collarbone.'

From the couch in the sheriff's office Clay Bogaine groaned as the little doctor bent over him. From the swivel-chair behind the desk Lobo Watkins said, 'I was scared too. He'll be more good to us alive than dead — we hope.'

His face liberally beplastered, Lobo looked like a clown. His one arm was bare: the doctor had torn away the sleeve in order to bandage the long nasty cut on the forearm. But at least Lobo had no broken bones.

Mike Daventry sat on the edge of the desk. 'Can you fix him, Doc?' he asked. 'He's our prisoner, yuh know. We aim to hold him for questioning anyway.'

'I can fix him.' The little doctor

smiled sardonically. 'I hope you find him a nice comfortable cell.'

'We'll do him proud,' said the sheriff.

The door opened and Sadie Cane came in. The golden-haired woman stood arms akimbo and surveyed the battered man behind the desk.

'Well, you crazy no-account coyote,' she said. 'So you're still alive.' Her voice dropped. 'You had me scared.'

'I had myself scared,' admitted Lobo. 'Bogaine's no prairie puff-ball. I've gotten a new respect for the man, even if he is a back-shooting skunk.'

Sadie crossed to the couch. 'Need any help, Doc?'

'Just a modicum, Sadie girl, thank you.'

The door opened again and Pegleg Brown, festooned with gunbelts, marched in. He stumped around the desk and slapped Lobo heartily on the shoulder.

'Hey, take it easy!'

'You suttingly are a ringtailed bobcat, pardner, you suttinly took that tiger by the tail — an' threw him through the window.' The old-timer went off into yelps of remembering laughter.

When the spasm was finished and he had got his breath back he said, 'That sidewinder ain't gonna die is he, Doc?'

'No, he'll be all right.'

'Pity!' Pegleg placed the gunbelts on the desk, made his *adios* and left.

When Clay Bogaine came round he was lying on a clean blanket on a fairly respectable bunk. But he was in a cell which was slowly beginning to fill with woolly darkness. He felt too weak to yell, so he lay and did some thinking. He wondered what Duke Roland would do about this sudden turn of events.

Had Clay been able to see Duke right then his thinking would have gotten even more tangled.

Duke had another minion who, at the moment, seemed to be taking Clay's place. This character was a lean fast-moving younker with a squint, a face as dark as any Indian's. He called himself Kid Moonlight. He was quick with wits, gun or knife and as deadly as a diamond-backed rattler. He had long coveted Clay's job as *segunda* of the boss.

He always acted as second in command when Clay was doing a special job on his own or was otherwise unavailable. So now he sat with Duke in the latter's luxurious little cabin on the edge of town and their heads were together and Duke talked fast.

Bogaine was not aware of this meeting of his two friends. But he became aware of the result of the meeting about two hours later as he lay on his bunk and dozed. It was just a sound at first and, of course, he could not know that this sound was the result of a meeting between two people he considered to be his friends, or at least his saddle-pards. But the sound became louder and deepened and he recognized it as the special awful sound made by the throats — like one collective animal throat — of a bloodlusting mob. Yes, he knew it; once he had led a mob like that himself. But still he could hardly believe his ears.

And the sound grew louder, swelled, and he knew his ears were not playing him false. Then he told himself that they couldn't be coming for him. Why would they come for him? They must be after somebody else. But there are some things that even a brave man cannot wait to know. He opened his mouth and yelled for the sheriff.

It was Lobo Watkins who came, however, and Bogaine wished he hadn't yelled.

Lobo lounged against the wall of the passage and said, 'The outraged populace are coming a-callin' on yuh, Clay. I suggest you tell us all about the attack on Jake Morgan, about the raid on the Craddock ranch and the murder of the four night-riders, and a few more things beside maybe. I've got more than a hunch that you're mixed up in it all. I guess if you talk fast we'll be able to save your neck.'

'Go to hell,' said Bogaine.

'Suit yourself.' Lobo lounged away down the passage.

Bogaine flogged his sluggish brain. Then he grinned in the darkness. Watkins thought he was smart. Clay saw it all now. The law had got their friends together and staged this mob. They thought if Clay got good and scared he'd talk. But Clay didn't scare easily.

The sounds outside were increasing in volume, savage, blood-chilling. Despite himself, Bogaine shivered. A voice above the rest screamed, 'Let's go get him.' They were certainly making things sound realistic.

There seemed a hell of a lot of them out there too. Then Bogaine had another brainwave. Maybe it was his own boys out there, creating a diversion so that they could bust him out. Watkins had just been acting cocky: he and the sheriff were the ones in the fix. Bogaine grinned again; trust Duke to think of something!

Lobo and Mike went out on to the

boardwalk in front of the office. They both carried loaded shotguns. At their appearance, the crowd's baying broke up into threats, jeers and catcalls.

'We want Bogaine,' yelled somebody.

Then a man in front of the crowd spoke up. 'Better let us through or it'll be the worse for you.'

'That's Kid Moonlight,' said the sheriff out of the corner of his mouth. 'He's supposed to be Bogaine's pal.'

'He looks a mean young cuss.'

'He is. If things come to the worst we'll blast the centre there around Kid. Seems to me all that bunch are so-called friends of Bogaine's.' Mike Daventry was acting like a real lawman now. His back to the wall, he sounded almost happy.

Lobo raised one hand. The growling of the crowd died a little. Lobo shouted, 'We give you fair warning. If you try to rush us we'll blast two gaps right through you.'

'They're bluffing,' yelled Kid Moonlight.

'You'll be the first, Kid,' shouted Mike Daventry.

'Maybe this is a put-up job,' said Lobo. 'Maybe they just want to set Bogaine free.'

'No, I don't think so. A lot of these people are just ordinary townsfolk who've been whipped into a frenzy and see a chance to get rid of at least one of the scum. Kid Moonlight and his boys have played along, pulling the wool over their eyes. Maybe it'd suit Kid to get Bogaine out of the way too.'

The crowd filled the street and flowed on to the sidewalk on the other side, a sea of howling faces, pressing forward so that for a moment it seemed that those in the front would be pushed into action whether they wished it or not. Kid Moonlight and his coherts had gotten themselves into a tight spot, probably much tighter than they had expected. The mob they had whipped into a frenzy had grown out of all proportion to its original size. Although many of those at the back were drunks having themselves a time and assorted females who didn't want to miss anything they added their weight to the press.

The Kid and his pals had no loophole through which they could squirm away, even gracelessly. It was a tradition of lawmen that they wouldn't shoot into a mob unless desperate, in case they hit innocent people, men, women or children who had been swept along in the general mêlée and ordinarily were decent citizens. But the Kid and his boys could not know whether the lawmen were bluffing or not and they hesitated. And while they hesitated the law was joined by reinforcements.

Sadie Cane and Pegleg Brown, both carrying shotguns, terrible weapons in the hands of experts, though far from being pea-shooters even in the hands of duffers. Lopez and three of his Mexican friends he had raked from a nearby cantina, all armed to the teeth. Then a gasp went up from the crowd as another woman put in an appearance, a rifle in the crook of her arm, Lucinda Sanders, joining her dark beauty to Sadie's golden presence. The law did a mite of gasping for itself at the sight of the lastcomer.

'He insisted it was time he took a walk,' said Lucinda.

Bruno Jensen grinned lopsidedly. A heavy Colt hung at the end of each of his long arms. He leaned against the door-jamb and lifted the guns and pointed them at the crowd and kept on grinning.

Kid Moonlight saw things were going all wrong and like a cornered rat went haywire.

'Rush 'em!' he screamed. 'Rush 'em!'

Lobo Watkins leaned his shotgun against the wall, crossed the boardwalk and stepped down. Kid Moonlight went for his gun, then screamed in agony as the toe of Lobo's boot bit into his elbow. His gun fell to the ground. Lobo grabbed him by a handful of shirt and dragged him on to the boardwalk.

A few people laughed. The temper of the mob was changing. The Kid's friends looked sullen and, in the face of a battery of guns, did nothing.

Lobo said to the sheriff, 'I'll take this coyote through to Bogaine and tell him what his friends were trying to do for him. Maybe he'll do some singing then.'

'Watch out,' screamed Sadie.

Lobo twisted. Kid Moonlight's knife missed his neck by a hairsbreadth. Lobo lashed out. The Kid took the blow full in the mouth. He crashed against the wall and slid down into a sitting position. His knife imbedded itself in the boards at his feet, quivered there. Lobo picked it up, noticed it was the twin of the one that had been used on Mad Jake. Kid Moonlight moaned feebly.

Lobo grabbed him by the scruff of the neck. The sheriff opened the office door and Lobo dragged the would-be lynch leader through. He was halfway across the office, dragging the Kid like a sack of meal, when the shot boomed from the back. Lobo dropped the Kid, whipped out his gun, ran.

The smell of powdersmoke filled the passage outside the cell-block. The lighted hurricane-lantern threw sparse rays through the bars of Bogaine's cell.

Bogaine was crumpled up at the foot of the barred door, as if he had been trying to claw his way out when his assassin shot him from the barred window. Cursing terribly, Lobo fumbled keys, got the door open. A heavy slug had made a mess of Bogaine's head. There was nothing Lobo could do for him.

Gun in hand, Lobo climbed on the bunk and looked through the window. There was just blackness and a breeze off the range. The sounds of the mob, dispersing now quite happily, came to him. They probably hadn't even heard the shot. It had all been so easy. All the killer had to do was climb on to his horse's saddle, fire through the window, lower himself into a sitting position again and ride away. Even if Bogaine had recognized his murderer he hadn't had a chance, he had been caught like a dog in a pit, shot down with less compunction than a mad dog.

Lobo went back into the passage, just in time to forestall a dash for freedom being made by Kid Moonlight. Not able to get out through the front, Kid was aiming for the back door. After receiving the barrel of Lobo's gun across the side of his head, the Kid decided to stay put.

Lobo dragged the body of Bogaine out of the cell and put the Kid in its place. He figured the Kid would keep for a while: the killer wasn't likely to come back, his turkey-shooting being finished for one night.

Lobo went back into the office to meet his partners and tell them the law's ace-in-the-hole had been transformed into a joker.

The news had a mixed reception.

'It looks like Kid Moonlight and his

friends won the game after all,' said the sheriff.

'That ain't gonna do Kid much good,' said Lobo. 'He's taking Bogaine's place.'

Bruno Jensen, sitting on the couch with his head against the wall, had quit grinning for a while. 'Poor Clay,' he said. 'So I made a trip down here for nothing. I was aiming to save him all for myself.'

'Well, can you beat that!' snorted Lobo. 'Won't this young hellion ever learn?'

He wondered privately whether Bruno had improved his draw any by his secret practising.

Lucinda sat down beside Bruno and put her arm around his shoulders. 'He's got to go right back to bed,' she said.

8

Even in a corner, Kid Moonlight proved to be a tougher rat than one might have expected. Threats left him unmoved. He had his story and he meant to stick to it. He had joined the lynch mob, he said, because he thought that in the ensuing mêlée he might be able to save his old saddle-pard Bogaine from them. Yes, Clay had been his friend. So why would he know anything about Clay's murder? If they tried to pin anything like that on him they would be the laughing-stock of Cravett: everybody knew he had been out front of the jail. Why, Lobo himself could have shot Bogaine — out of sheer spite probably . . .

This squint-eyed little rat was in the power of Lobo. But he was in the power of the law too, and the law was fair and just (at least, the kind of law Lobo believed in): Lobo stopped short at actual violence to the man in the cell. Kid Moonlight sensed his captor's strange idealism and mocked it and took advantage of it. He said the law couldn't hold him. He had only been one of a mob. If they wanted to hold him they'd have to lock up most of the rest of the town too.

The following morning in the drizzling rain another man put in an appearance at the jail. Lobo had heard of him, had seen him around, and half-expected to see him turn up now. He was a dried-up shyster lawyer named Isaac Rooke, a friend of Duke Roland's — or, at least, one of that great man's sycophants. He brought with him a writ of some kind. Lobo didn't quite understand it but Sheriff Daventry said it was legal all right and it meant they'd have to let the prisoner go.

This was one time Lobo regretted he had elected to be a law officer and wear a tin star. He would like to toss this little dried-up cuss into the horse-trough down the street and then take Kid Moonlight out back somewhere and beat the truth out of him.

But he obeyed Mike Daventry and let the sneering young hardcase go.

Strangely enough, as the office door closed behind the two men Lobo was smiling wickedly. 'I've got an idea,' he said. 'Maybe just a hunch.'

'What's that?' said old Mike glumly.

'That knife the Kid tried to cut me with last night, it was the same as was used on Jake Morgan. I vote that after we have let the Kid blow his feathers out for a while we'll pull him in again on suspicion of doing that job. Jake's dead, remember. Leastways, I hope everybody thinks so.'

'Hundreds of those knives are sold,' said Mike. 'The chandler down the road sells them.'

'Maybe he'll be able to give me some information,' said Lobo. 'I'll go down there.'

Yes, the storekeeper sold a lot of

those knives, but he couldn't remember who he sold them to. He couldn't remember ever having sold one to Kid Moonlight. He was a shifty-eyed character, very unco-operative. Lobo wondered whether he was another of those who preyed on his fellow townsmen. He might even be one of the night riders. It was getting so that Lobo suspected everybody of being in league against law and order. He wanted to grab the man by his scrawny Adam's apple and shake him. But he remembered the tin star and he turned and walked out of the stores.

He went on to Sadie's place. As he entered the saloon somebody hailed him. Bruno Jensen sat at a corner table with a bottle and glass in front of him. 'Sit down and have a drink,' he invited.

'Later,' said Lobo. 'How do you feel?'

'Fine.'

'Well, don't get sticking your neck out.'

'You know me, boss.'

'That's just the point.'

Lobo went on and up the stairs.

Over coffee he told Sadie and Lucinda the latest news. Lucinda seemed more worried about Bruno than about Kid Moonlight having escaped the net.

'Bruno's all right,' Lobo told her. 'A bellyfull of rotgut ain't gonna hurt him. He's celebrating being a whole man again, I guess.' He knew Bruno was unpredictable but he wasn't going to admit this to Lucinda.

'It's time you two went back to the ranch,' he went on. 'Bruno's plenty fit enough to travel.'

'He says he aims to stay here until you leave.'

'He'll obey orders.' Lobo hoped his voice carried conviction.

Sadie told what she knew about the forming of the lynch mob, which wasn't much. She had been having a bath when she heard the shindig downstairs. By the time she got down there most of the mob was streaming down the street.

Lucinda and Bruno had joined her

and they had got ready for action. The rest Lobo knew.

'Billy the barman or old Pegleg might be able to tell you more,' Sadie added.

Pegleg was sent for. But he was of no more help. He had been delivering a bottle of wine to a sick friend and the mob was well under way when he got back. He had been just in time to join Sadie and the rest of the rescue party, that was all.

'Do any of you remember seeing Duke Roland that night?' asked Lobo.

'I didn't,' said Sadie. 'He wasn't in the bar-room when I looked down there and he certainly wouldn't mingle with the mob. Not Duke!'

None of the others had seen him either. They trooped downstairs to confab with Billy the barman. He didn't remember having seen Duke either.

'Was it Kid Moonlight who got the mob going?' Lobo asked him now.

'All that bunch seemed to be doing a lot of spouting,' said the barman. 'But the actual mob didn't seem to form in here, more out on the sidewalk. It seemed to me that it had all been fixed beforehand by the rough element.'

Lobo let it go at that. He thought about seeking Duke Roland out, even arresting him on suspicion. But he soon realized that he had not an atom of proof that, although Kid Moonlight was one of Duke's cohorts, Duke had been behind the lynch mob or the murder of Bogaine. Why would Duke want Bogaine killed, this man who was supposed to have been his friend? Had he been scared that Bogaine would crack and give things away, so had killed him to shut his mouth for good? If such was the case it was a crime committed by a man who might himself be cracking, who had got to the point where he couldn't afford to trust anybody.

But Roland was still a force in Cravett. A force for evil, a figurehead.

The quickest solution to everything, Lobo thought, was to pick a fight with

Roland and cut him down. Roland was quite a hellcat by all accounts and the fastest man in the territory with a shooting-iron. That would be some fight. Lobo grinned wolfishly as he thought of it. But he knew that this solution was one which he as a peace officer could not yet follow. Despite the fact that he knew Roland to be a villain, Lobo couldn't tackle him until he had some kind of count against him.

But there were other people who figured they had a few counts against Roland. They didn't put in an appearance till the evening and, in the meantime Lobo Watkins made a few more enquiries which got him exactly no-place.

He was grieved to discover that Jake Morgan was still only semi-conscious at intervals and no more coherent. The ox-like man wasn't pulling out of things very quickly. Lobo consulted Doc Masters.

'I confess he puzzles me,' said the

little doctor. 'It's almost as if he doesn't want to get well, as if something back there in his mind is telling him not to.'

'You mean he's going really crazy after all?'

'No, not exactly.' Masters smiled thinly. 'I believe Jake's craziness was just an act with him. He liked being called Mad Jake, behind his back, of course. He liked to stand this town on its head from time to time. He's one of the old plainsmen who hates people in the mass. He hates towns like this and the kind of people they spawn. He liked to show his contempt of it all from time to time. The way people laughed at him was nothing to the way he must have been laughing at them. For there was fear in their laughter and never any fear in his. In his way he exploited this town . . . '

The doctor's voice trailed off and Lobo said, 'You sort of drop in to talking about Jake as if he was already dead. Do you think . . . '

'I don't know, Lobo.' The doctor

shook his head slowly from side to side. 'I don't know.'

'But why would a man like Jake *want* to die? I've known old Jake for years — although I ain't actually seen him for such a long time. I'll tell you something, Doc.' Lobo's voice was almost desperate.

'I was with him in the war between the States. I was just a drummer-boy, a skinny little orphan. He was our company scout. I thought more of him than all the goddamned officers put together. He was like a father to me. I'd never known my own father and I hadn't seen my mother in years. The drummer-boy was fair game for some of the dumb old soldiers, but Jake soon put a stop to that. I grew; we served together for years, we escaped death together, raised hell together. Nobody wanted to live more than Jake did. And now you tell me . . . '

Words failed Lobo for a moment. Then he burst out again: 'Gosh, he knows I'm here, he knows I'll stand by him whatever . . . '

'Perhaps he's forgotten you're here,' said Doc Masters. 'Perhaps he's forgotten everything but that little something in the back of his mind which is telling him not to get well. Perhaps Mad Jake, as we've called him, is a man with a secret.'

'You talk in riddles, Doc.'

The little man shrugged. 'Perhaps I do. I'm only an obscure cow town sawbones. There are lots of things I don't understand, that I can only grope for. There are lots of things in the human system, the human mind which baffle even the greatest ones of my profession.' He shrugged again, made a little eloquent gesture with his pudgy hands. He sounded resigned. At that moment Lobo could have struck him. But he realized that nothing was the doctor's fault, the doctor was a good man.

Lobo was not a particularly well-educated man. He thought that even the doctor had plumbed depths which he could never reach. Strange thoughts spun around in his mind. What secret could a man like Jake Morgan have? It was ludicrous: Lobo almost laughed aloud.

But his mind would not let the thought go. If Jake had a secret, and he lived, would he tell Lobo that secret?

★   ★   ★

If the townsfolk of Cravett remembered that only last night they had been screaming like animals for a man's blood they quickly pushed the thought to the backs of their minds. But because of this they were all the more boisterous and friendly and open-handed on the following night. They still spoke of Bogaine but most of them as if he had been a good friend of theirs and they had never wished him any harm, that they had only gone along last night because they had heard the shindig and wondered what was happening. Some of them pretended that they hadn't been there at all. It was a wonder how a lynch mob had ever been formed. Who could have killed Clay, they asked. Speculation was rife.

Sadie moved among her customers in the old way, smiling and nodding, her eyes watchful. She was superbly dressed in a tight wine-red gown which set off her golden beauty. Her hair was elaborately curled and piled on top of her head and fastened with a black comb in which red stones glittered beneath the lights. She was so different from the wild-looking yellow-haired filly, locks streaming in the wind, who had ridden with King Craddock on that fateful day not so very long ago.

Now there was another King in Cravett territory and he was holding court now at a big round table in a corner of the bar-room. How long would it be before Duke Roland (why didn't he call himself King now and go the whole hog?) was toppled from *his* throne? Sadie shuddered a little as she thought of how it would be possible to bring about the downfall of her enemy. One man could possibly do it. He would do it if she asked him to. But her hardness was marshmallow now and she knew that, because slip-ups *could* happen, she would never ask.

The Duke was playing cards with his courtiers, with Kid Moonlight by his side and the rest grouped around him, about eight of them. There were others of his hangers-on at nearby tables. They all seemed pleased with themselves. Things were boisterous up there and even Duke was grinning, his sallow face unwontedly flushed.

In the opposite corner of the room a small band played. Piano, bull-fiddle, squeeze-box and cornet. Some of the percentage-girls were dancing with the boys but space was limited. The bar was doing a rip-roaring trade, the chips clicked, the roulette wheels spun, the croupiers intoned the odds. Men laughed and yelled and sang, girls shrieked and giggled shrilly. There was a note of hysterical gaiety about the scene. People kept coming in.

It was getting late. At first people hardly noticed the final batch of newcomers. Then a ripple ran round the room and things became a little less noisy.

The tall thin man shouldered his way towards the bar. His was a hard-bitten face. He turned it neither to left or right and yet he appeared quite nonchalant.

He was George Pinfold, ramrod of the Craddock ranch and behind him more of the Craddock boys, as well as some hard-looking characters people didn't remember having seen before.

Closest to Pinfold was a big man who walked with a lopsided gait as if one of his shoulders was lower than the other. There was a scar on his face which gave him a perpetual leering expression, as if he didn't like what he saw of Cravett and was soundlessly laughing at it all. One or two folks recognized him, just the way Lobo Watkins had recognized him when he saw him at the ranch a few days before. His name was whispered around the saloon. He was Amos Moon, a notorious gunfighter and killer who hailed from the hellhole of the Pecos.

The Craddock boys had always been a pretty tough bunch and a rumour had got around recently that George Pinfold had brought gunnies in to top them off. Here was proof that this was no wild rumour. They were here in force too, though they didn't seem to be looking for trouble — yet.

They ranged themselves along the bar. People made way for them. Barmen took their orders courteously. Sadie said 'Howdy' to George Pinfold who was, indeed, an old friend of hers. And then she continued on her rounds as if there was nothing strange about George being here right now.

Craddock men exchanged greetings with townsfolk they knew, though it was with a certain wariness on the part of the latter. The strangers, hard-bitten characters to the last man, were quite affable too. They drank steadily, as if that was all they had come to Cravett for. And why not? The band played, the gaming went on, men shouted and women squealed, things went on as before, the last mad whirl before turning out.

Half an hour or so passed. Amos Moon stood at the bar next to a little fat man who kept a general store down the street. They exchanged desultory conversation. Then suddenly Moon raised his voice, a high, nasal, penetrating sort of voice.

'You know who I am don't yuh?'

'I can't say I do, suh,' said the little storeman, who hadn't heard the whispers that went around.

Moon became truculent. He hadn't been there long enough to imbibe a lot of liquor but he sounded drunk. Maybe he had had some someplace else. 'You're just saying that,' he hollered. 'You know who I am all right.'

'I assure you, suh . . . '

The rest of the little man's words were choked off as a big hand grabbed his collar, half-throttling him, lifting him up so that he teetered on his toes.

Moon's face twisted fearsomely, his scar writhing like a living thing, obscene. 'My name's Amos Moon,' he hollered. 'I eat a little pipsqueak like you for breakfast every morning. But I'll let you go if you tell me one thing.'

The little man twisted his head as much as he was able, his face going slowly purple. All he saw was grinning faces, many belonging to people he had short-changed, who enjoyed his misfortune.

'What?' he gasped. 'What do you want to know?'

'I am looking for a filthy skunk who calls himself Duke Roland,' hollered Moon. 'He was responsible for the death of a dear friend of mine, pore young Cal Jensen. If I meet that stinking scheming coyote who calls himself Duke,' Moon brayed with laughter, 'I'm gonna fill him so full o' lead that he'll bury himself.' He shook his victim violently. 'Where's he hang

139

out, little man? Tell me. Where's Duke Roland?'

The storeman rolled his head from side to side, gurgling, his eyes popping from his head. He had little chance to tell where Duke Roland was. But other people were looking towards the corner and Duke was rising, for, natural actor that he was, he could do nothing else. He moved away from the table and his voice rang out.

'If you're looking for Duke Roland, here he is!'

Moon sent the little storeman skittling away from him and turned away from the bar. There was a wild scurry as people scattered in all directions. Moon went forward to meet Roland.

Duke saw his man clearly now. He had thought him to be a drunken lout but now he realized different. He was a practised gunfighter who knew what he was doing. And he was cold-sober too. It had been an act. This had all been fixed.

Duke's men were rising, only to find

themselves already covered by guns in the hands of Craddock men. Sadie Cane gave a little gasp of indignation and started forward, only to pull up short as something hard nudged her in the back. She turned, looked up into the cold eyes of her old friend, George Pinfold, looked down at the colt George held in his hand.

'I'd do it,' said George softly. 'Even to you, Sadie. This time Duke Roland's gonna get what's coming to him.'

9

Sheriff Daventry and Lobo Watkins were playing cards in the sheriff's office. On the desk between them was a bottle of best bonded whiskey and two tumblers. The old pot-bellied stove hummed drowzily and glowed with warmth. From down the street from time to time came gusts of revelry as the batwings of Sadie's place swung to and fro.

'Whooping it up ain't they?' said the sheriff.

'I wonder if they would have been the same had they strung Bogaine up last night,' said Lobo. 'Or would most of these hell-snorting townsfolk have skulked at home, avoiding each other's eyes. Maybe it's a good thing somebody *did* shoot Bogaine, it's a salve to the consciences of some of that scum. I support the next thing they'll be hooting for is the one who killed their poor old friend Clay.'

'You're a cynic, Lobo,' said Mike Daventry.

'Why, ain't you?'

'I ain't got the savvy left to be anything in particular,' said Mike glumly.

'Here, snap out of it!' Lobo slammed a card down on the desk. 'Beat that one if you can.'

Mike essayed a grin. 'I cain't do it. You're a real sharpy, you are, ain't yuh?'

Horses went by outside at a walking pace, seemed to be heading out of town. The sound died in the distance, but almost immediately there was the thundering of more hoofs down the street, coming faster. But the sound stopped almost as suddenly as it had begun. The stove puffed gently, there was peace and warmth in the little office. But neither of the men seemed to be concentrating now on their game or their liquor.

'Sounded like that bunch stopped at

Sadie's place,' said Mike.

'A sizeable bunch too by the sound of it,' said Lobo.

'I can only think of one bunch who'd ride in force like that,' said Mike.

Both men rose, skirted the desk. The office door crashed open and two men entered, guns in their hands. Lobo's hand dropped instinctively to his belt, although there was no gun there.

'Freeze it,' snarled a voice behind him. 'Unless you want a hole in your spine.'

One of the men in front kicked the door to behind him with his heel. 'Get your hands up.'

Lobo raised his hands, saw that Mike was doing the same. He glanced over his shoulder. Two more men had come through the door which led into the cell block. One of these was the would-be spine-plugging character.

'Never leave your back door unlocked,' sniggered one of the men.

'Ain't I seen you at the Craddock place?' said the sheriff mildly.

'Shut your trap, old-timer,' said the man, 'or I'll bend this gun over your skull.'

'Move together,' said one of the men by the door.

Mike and Lobo did as they were told. They had no option, particularly in view of the fact that their gunbelts hung over a chair yards away from them.

'Turn around!'

They complied.

The two men fanned away from the door of the cell block.

'March!'

Mike and Lobo marched. One of the men grabbed the keys from Mike's belt. Next moment the two lawmen were locked in one of their own cells.

The four visitors moved away. With a laugh, one of them threw the bunch of keys into the passage. They fell against the wall on the opposite side to the cell, well out of the reach of the imprisoned lawmen.

'If you holler we'll come back and shut you up for good,' was the threat.

The door slammed. There was silence.

'Everything happens to us,' groaned Mike.

But Lobo had already climbed on to the bunk and was looking through the barred window. He couldn't see a thing. He got down again and began to prowl around the cell like a caged beast. Mike revolved slowly, watching him and finally said, 'You might as well set and make the most of it, son.'

He suited the action to the words and sat down on the bunk with a sigh of resignation. 'Cain't think why they want to coop us up in here,' he said.

'Maybe they want to blow the place up and us with it,' said Lobo sardonically.

He came to a halt in front of Mike, hands on hips, feet planted wide apart, head thrust forward at a predatory angle.

'There's somethin' goin' on down-town an' they don't want us in on it,' he said softly.

'A raid!'

Mike rose again, shaking his lethargy from him. Lobo turned away from him and went across to the cell door. Mike joined him and they stood there side by side gazing at the bunch of keys on the other side of the passage.

Then it was Mike's turn to rove around the cell. 'If only we could find something to reach 'em.'

'Wait a minute,' said Lobo and almost knocked him over.

He raked blankets and palliasse from the bunk. Mike joined him. Finally, making as little noise as possible in case one of the nocturnal visitors was on guard outside, they managed to get the bunk down. They tore a lath from it, liberally besplintering their fingers in the process. They took the lath over to the barred door and began to fish.

It was not as easy as one might have expected. The lath was thick and cumbersome and made quite a lot of clatter. The men cursed savagely, softly. The keys could not be hooked, the lath was too big for that; they could only be scraped along the floor. This was surprisingly difficult, almost impossible. When the lath touched the keys all it seemed to do was make them chink alarmingly.

The two men cursed and struggled, taking it in turns, making savage suggestions to each other as if they were sworn enemies. Although the night was quite cool, sweat began to run down their faces.

The door at the end of the passage opened and one of the gunmen came along. 'Back!' he snarled. 'You've been warned.'

The two lawmen backed from the menace of the gun. The gunman leered, there was death in his eyes and he enjoyed their discomfiture. He bent to pick up the keys. Lobo charged, the wooden lath held in front of him like a lance. It shot through the bars and speared the gunman with terrible force on the side of the jaw, slamming him against the wall. His gun clattered away out of sight along the passage. He slid to a recumbent heap against the wall, plumb on top of the keys. He was dead to the world.

'Cripes,' moaned Mike Daventry. 'Now we've got to shift *him* as well.'

★   ★   ★

Pegleg Brown and Bruno Jensen, like Sadie, both had guns ground into their backs by Craddock men. They could only stand and watch the scene that went on in the centre of the saloon.

Bruno only hoped that Lucinda did not take it into her head to come downstairs right then.

The hush was portentous; the band had dried-up, chips no longer clicked, roulette wheels no longer hummed and chattered. Even the blue smoke around the lights and under the rafters seemed to be hanging motionless as if waiting. The only sound was the slow almost imperceptible scrape of the feet of Amos Moon and Duke Roland.

George Pinfold had one eye on Sadie

and one eye on Billy behind the bar. One of George's men had taken charge of Billy's shotgun, but there were plenty of heavy bottles and whatnots nearby which the barman could conceivably use as weapons.

'Get him, Amos,' hissed George. The words were hardly audible but the sound carried in the quiet.

Even so it was doubtful if Amos Moon heard anything. He only had eyes for the man in front of him, this man who, despite his foppish appearance looked like he might be able to handle himself.

He saw a tall man in black broadcloth with lean sallow features and cold snake-like eyes, the eyes of a killer.

'Make your play, friend,' said Duke Roland softly and Amos realized that this man wasn't scared, he wasn't scared a bit.

Pinfold had said this Cravett big-shot, this man who called himself Duke, was no easy meat, but Amos had laughed at him. So many men had gone down before the Pecos killer's blazing guns.

But Amos wasn't laughing now, though his scar made him appear to be doing so. There was something about this character . . . he was as cold as a fish — but he was no fish. A little cold doubt niggled at the back of Amos's mind. But he shook it away from him, watching the man's eyes as a gunfighter must watch his opponent's eyes, waiting for that tell-tale flicker which often came before the downward swoop of the hand.

But Duke's eyes were like small cold marbles beneath lowered lids. They did not flicker but a little flame lay deep in them, the light of pure evil.

Then Duke moved and Amos made a jerky draw. He'd never made a draw like that before and in that split second he knew he was finished. His gun was in his hand but he could not seem to lift it and flame beat in his chest and exploded in his brain and he was falling.

He was dead before he struck the floor.

George Pinfold cursed vilely, started forward. Sadie Cane twisted, catlike. She grabbed George's arm. His gun went off, the slug burying itself in the floor. George, tripped by Sadie, fell flat on his face.

The man who guarded Billy the barman's shotgun turned abruptly to try and help his boss. In one smooth movement Billy grabbed a bottle, swung it, burst it over the man's head. The Craddock man folded up over the footrail. Billy leaned over the bar and grabbed his shotgun, swung it up.

'All right . . . '

He ducked as somebody took a shot at him. The mirror behind him was starred. Then somebody shot the lights out and place was suddenly plunged into stygian darkness.

There was no more shooting, friend was scared of plugging friend. There was a lot of thudding and scuffling and groaning and yelling and screaming.

The Craddock men were using their drawn guns with stunning effect.

'The door,' yelled somebody. 'Don't let 'em get away. They . . . '

The voice died away in a choking gurgle and shortly after that hoofs thudded in the street and died away in the distance.

Lights were found. The only member of the Craddock clan who remained was the unconscious man draped across the footrail. Even George Pinfold had managed to crawl out somehow. Amos Moon didn't count as any kind of man anymore. He was deader than mackerel and kind of mussed too.

By the time Mike and Lobo got there, after almost crippling themselves in getting the keys and unlocking their cell door, it was all over bar the shouting and there wasn't much of that. The law had two prisoners, both unconscious. One in the saloon and one in the jail block. And there was another case for the undertaker.

There were no serious injuries among

the townsfolk. Duke Roland had gone back to his card game. He had killed in self-defence. The Pecos killer had called him out and Duke had cut him down. Amos Moon was no loss to anybody. It had been a fair fight: the lawmen were told this over and over.

'Much as I'd like to see you clap that fancy jasper in jail, Lobo,' said Pegleg Brown. 'I gotta admit it was all fair. That Moon character was sent here to kill Duke and he pulled a boner. He only got what he was asking for.'

10

When the two Craddock men came to their senses they were in a cell together. One had a swollen jaw, the other a slightly cracked pate. Otherwise they were all right. Doc Masters patched them up, then handed them over to the tender mercies of Lobo Watkins.

As it happened, Lobo didn't have to hold any threats over their heads. They were new men, they didn't aim to stick their necks out for the Craddock ranch. They had been friends of Amos Moon and they knew what had happened to him. This was a tough town and they wanted no more part of it. They told Lobo they had been hired by George Pinfold, through Amos Moon. Pinfold had wanted extra men, preferably men who could handle their guns. He had offered them, through Amos, three times as much as the average cowhand's pay, with a big bonus at the end of the job. He hadn't said what the job might be but they had figured it certainly wouldn't be punching cows.

'We had our orders from Amos tonight,' said one of them. 'All we had to do was to stop anyone interfering in the fight between Amos an' this Duke feller. Amos was the only one who was supposed to do any shooting.' The man laughed harshly. 'Boy, did he pick himself a humdinger!'

Lobo said: 'We're gonna keep you here for a while. If we find out you're telling the truth we'll probably let you go, as long as you get clean out of this territory.'

'We'll do that,' they agreed fervently.

The following morning Mike Daventry said: 'D'you think we ought to ride out to the Craddock place? Legally we ain't got much on 'em, I guess.'

'Maybe we ought to let 'em simmer a while then,' said Lobo. 'Seems to me we ain't done much towards finding out who tried to rustle their cattle and who killed their four night-riders.'

'I guess we *know* who was behind that,' said Mike. 'But finding proof is a different thing.'

'Today's the day fixed for Mad Jake's funeral,' said Lobo. He smiled thinly; the smile did not reach his eyes. He was hoping that the mockery would not become a reality and Mad Jake had to have two funerals: one pretence, one real. The old buzzard was still in a bad way: like Doc Masters had said, he didn't seem as if he wanted to live.

'That'd be a signal to rake Kid Moonlight in again too,' added Lobo softly. 'Remember that knife?'

'We wouldn't be able to make it stick,' said Mike.

'Maybe not. But we might be able to scare Kid into talking.'

'He doesn't scare easy . . . '

'Or scare somebody else into giving themselves away.'

'If you're thinking about Duke

Roland, he ain't got a scare in him.'

'You should know,' said Lobo, and saw Mike wince, and wished he had kept his mouth shut.

But this lawman business was beginning to get on Lobo's nerves. This cat and mouse business, this investigating when there was nothing to investigate, this thought at the back of his mind all the time that while he sloped around playing the big law-shooter somebody laughed like hell behind his back. More than once he had been tempted to throw his little tin star in the gutter and start out and *make* himself some action. Besides, he had his ranch back home to think of . . .

He knew, however, that if he handed in his star he would be letting his old pard Mike down with a collossal bump, a bump from which the old man might never again recover. The law had begun to mean something — something maybe more precious than life — to the old mossy-horn again. That was why Lobo could not hand in his star; that was why Lobo could not take the law into his own hands and hell everything up.

But he did wish Mike wouldn't bellyache so much.

He followed Mike and they went to join the cortège which would wind its way up Boot Hill lamenting the late Mad Jake Morgan.

It was a real old-Western funeral, the kind Jake would have loved could he have seen it. Maybe he would've wanted to shoot it up. But only the chosen few knew that Jake, eyes closed, was continuing with his crazy muttering, so pitiful after the crazy laughter that had terrorized Cravett, as he lay on his bunk in the cubby-hole in the back of the livery-stable, watched over by Lopez and his boy. Only the chosen few knew that the coffin that was borne solemnly along the main drag was half full of pebbles and sand, packed down so that nothing could rattle. The bearers were Lobo, Mike, Doc Masters and three townsmen who claimed to have been friends of Jake. They were three fairly respectable middle-aged characters, certainly not Duke Roland men. Seemed like none of the tough element, or others, suspected they were being hoaxed.

Yes, a real old-Western funeral, with the mourners pacing slowly and not a horse in sight. There were plenty of mourners, townsfolk and children and assorted cats and curs streaming along behind and a watery sun shining down on it all. And Preacher Holmes leading the way and looking very self-important, reaching the open grave before anyone else and turning and standing there waiting with his hands folded over his good book and his eyes upturned solemnly like the eyes of dead fish.

The coffin was lowered laboriously into the grave. It was a big grave to take a big casket. 'Gosh,' gasped one sweating townsman. 'Jake was a giant, but I didn't figure him to be this heavy.'

'Maybe they left his spurs on,' said

another. 'Or fastened a gallon jar of rotgut up in there.'

He subsided, muttering to himself as the law and the doctor glared at him. Although the disgruntled townsmen didn't know it, those three jaspers were playing their sorrowing mourners' roles to the hilt.

Preacher Holmes intoned the burial service. The first clods fell on the coffin. A light rain began to fall, whispering as if in benediction. The grave was soon covered. The mourners returned slowly to town, many to Sadie's place to wash away the thought of death, but Mike and Lobo with sorrowful mein back to their office. Not until the street was fairly quiet again did these two reappear and make their way desultorily to the livery-stables. There a few minutes later Doc Masters joined them. Lopez stood at the door keeping watch, looking, as usual, half asleep. His little Mexican sidekick went round the back and pitched hay, but his little shoe-button eyes were keeping watch too.

Inside Mad Jake still moaned and muttered while Doc Masters took his pulse and looked puzzled.

After a moment Lobo Watkins said, 'Let me talk to him, Doc. I'm his oldest friend here. We've been through hell and heaven together. Maybe I can penetrate his consciousness.'

'He's in a fever,' said the doctor. 'Even a slight shock might prove fatal.'

'We've got to try something,' said Lobo desperately.

The little man stood up, stepped aside. 'He's all yours, my boy,' he said softly.

Lobo went down on one knee before the sick man. 'Jake,' he said softly but clearly. 'It's Lobo. It's ol' Lobo . . . '

Jake's head rolled, he muttered something inaudible.

'Jake,' said Lobo. 'Jake, honah . . . '

He lapsed into the sweet cajoling Texas drawl, the language that Jake understood and loved, the language of the plains and canyons of his home-lands, the language of the tall men, the soft-talking men, the hell-raising men. To the watchers, the listeners, there seemed nothing strange about a man calling another man 'honah'. A Texan man would say that to a friend. He would call a friend lots of other names too, but he would say that.

'Stir your bones, honah, you-all ain't daid yit. Remember the old days, Jake. This is Lobo, Jake. Remember Lobo and the old days . . . '

The man on the bunk began to struggle a little. His eyes opened but he didn't seem to see anything. Lobo leaned forward till their faces almost touched. 'Jake,' he whispered. 'It's your old saddle-pard, Lobo. The sassy drummer-boy, remember? It's Lobo, Jake — wake up, you old hoss.'

'Lobo,' Jake repeated the name over weakly like a sick child reciting a lesson.

Somebody moved slightly. Lobo flapped a hand impatiently, desperately. 'Jake! Listen to me, Jake. Remember the way you useter fight, you wuz the fightingest rooster thet iver wuz. You gotta fight now like you never fought before. I'm a-waiting for yuh, Jake — I'm countin' on yuh. It's gonna be jest the way it useter be — no matter what, it's gonna be jest the way it useter be. You hear me, Jake, this is Lobo talking to yuh. This is Lobo . . . ' Insistent, cajoling.

'Lobo,' the voice echoed, a little stronger now.

'Jake, honah, you're trying. I knew you wouldn't let yore ol' saddle-pard down . . . '

'Lobo . . . ' The eyes opened, seeking, a flicker of recognition in them now. The big hands groped. Lobo caught them. 'I'll help yuh, Jake. Remember how you useter help me? You ain't gonna give all that up.'

'Give him this,' whispered the doctor.

Lobo reached out behind him and took the cup of pale milky liquid. 'Drink this, old-timer,' he said, and held the cup to Jake's lips in the flaming red beard which still looked so much alive on the gaunt face.

Jake managed to raise his head a little. He took the liquid down. Then he sank back on the pillow with a little sigh and closed his eyes.

Doc Masters joined Lobo, gripped the young man's shoulder in a gesture of pleasure and congratulation. 'He's gone off to sleep like a child,' whispered the little man. 'I think he's going to be all right. An old friend's voice in the dark is sometimes better than all the doctor's medicine in the world. You were right, son, you were right.'

Lobo and the sheriff left the livery-stables and parted. Lobo went along to Sadie's place. Most of the funeral cortége had by now imbibed sufficiently and gone back to their chores. But a few barflies still drowsed in corners, or were draped untidily over the bar.

Lobo couldn't see anybody he knew very well. He went over to a clear part of the bar. The barman joined him. Lobo asked in a low voice, 'Has Kid Moonlight been in this morning?'

'Nope,' said the man. 'But I saw him

ride out of town with Duke Roland some time ago — just before the funeral it was.'

'Oh, I see.'

'D'yuh want a drink?'

'Not yet, thanks. See you later.'

Lobo turned away from the bar and almost ran into Pegleg Brown. Again he refused a drink. He promised to see Pegleg later and asked if Bruno Jensen was upstairs.

Pegleg said he figured Bruno was. Lobo climbed the stairs. In the passage he ran into Sadie.

'You come up for a cup of coffee, honey?' she asked.

'I want to see Bruno first. I'll come to the kitchen afterwards.' He planted a resounding kiss full on her lips. 'Will that hold you for a while?'

Sadie blushed. In her white shirtwaist and black skirt she looked like a beautiful schoolgirl.

'You'll have to do better than that,' she said and swayed into his arms.

After a time they broke apart and

Sadie hurried on to the kitchen, ostensibly to make coffee, but to tidy herself up too.

Lobo knocked on Bruno's door and opened it. Bruno was fully-dressed, even to hat and gunbelt. He turned guiltily, dropping his gun back into its holster when he saw who his visitor was. Evidently he had been practising his draw again.

'Uh, howdy, Lobo. I was just coming down. How about a drink?'

'I've promised Sadie I'll go an' have coffee with her in a few minutes. But I wanted to see you first.'

The two men stood looking at each other, neither of them electing to sit down. 'What's the matter, boss?' said Bruno. 'Have I done somep'n I shouldn't?'

'Gosh, no, you wouldn't be my foreman if you were in the habit o' doing things you shouldn't, you know that. However,' Lobo seemed to be weighing his words carefully, 'you do seem to stick your neck out when you ain't got any cows or cowpunchers to ride herd on. You're fit now an' you'll be needed back at the ranch. I wanted you an' Lucinda to pack your traps an' leave on the next stage.'

'Oh — uh. You want to get rid o' me! An' you think I'll just light out an' leave you in this den o' prairie wolves? After you came because of me, too. What kind of a skunk do you take me for?'

'Don't be silly. There's no question of you lighting out. You're needed back at the ranch. Besides, Lucinda won't leave until you do an' you can't keep her here indefinitely, old Buck'll be wondering what's happened to her.'

'He won't. She sent him a wire yesterday.'

'Oh, hell, you're just being obstreperous. I'll be leaving here myself purty soon now.'

'All right then, seein' as it won't be long, we might as well wait for you — company for the journey y'know . . . '

'I order you to go back to the ranch,' snapped Lobo. Bruno drew himself up to the full height of his lean, gangling frame. His mild, pale eyes had an indignant look about them. He took off his hat slowly and tossed it on the bed. He had slicked back his tow hair with some fixative he had bought from the local barber's shop and now the room stank of the stuff.

Bruno was a picture of outraged dignity . . . Then, slowly, he began to grin.

'Shucks, boss,' he said. 'You wouldn't want to bust me an' Lucinda right up, would yuh? Lucinda says she ain't leaving here till you leave. You know Lucinda, she's a mighty strong-willed little filly. If she says she's staying, wild horses wouldn't drag her away.'

Despite himself, Lobo grinned too. 'You're just making that up,' he said.

'You go see Lucinda then,' said Bruno, neatly passing the buck.

'I'll do that,' said Lobo and turned on his heel.

Bruno grinned at the closed door.

Then he drew his gun and spun it by the trigger-guard. He missed a spin, dropped the gun, cursed.

'I'll go get myself a drink,' he said aloud. He picked up the gun, pouched it, left the room.

Meanwhile, Lobo had cornered Lucinda in the kitchen, where she was helping Sadie.

Lucinda gave him the same answer as Bruno had done.

'You can't expect us to leave, Lobo,' she said. 'You know that.'

Lobo confessed himself beaten. 'All right,' he said. 'But try and keep that sassy boy-friend of yours out of trouble, will you?'

'I'll try.'

They sat down to coffee and hot cakes dispensed by the smiling Sadie. 'Maybe we'll all light out together,' she said, and Lobo wondered what she meant by that.

After a while he took himself off downstairs. Pegleg Brown was no longer in sight. Neither was anybody else Lobo knew except the barman. Lobo did not see Bruno seated in a dim corner with a bottle of whiskey and a glass.

Lobo crossed to the bar, decided he'd take just one drink to top off the coffee and cakes. The barman served him. Lobo took the tot, half-turned with it in his hand, rested his elbow on the bar, one foot on the brass footrail. Kid Moonlight came swaggering through the batwings.

The Kid saw Lobo, and some of his swank left him. He paused as if he would retreat. But he changed his mind and came on again. It was Kid's boast that he wasn't scared of anybody. Nobody disputed this. Maybe he had thought it wasn't really expedient that he should meet Lobo now. But there was no hope for it.

'Red-eye, Billy,' he sang out. He had decided he would act as if Lobo just wasn't there.

But Lobo had been doing some fast thinking too. He had been half-inclined to let the Kid simmer a bit longer. But he didn't like the Kid's attitude, shifty and yet lordly, as if he had weighed things up and figured that Lobo just couldn't touch him. Lobo was thoroughly antagonized now by the Kid's imperious back. The Kid was still wanted for questioning, even though a shyster lawyer had got him off once. Now was as good a time as any to pull the Kid in.

Lobo walked along the bar. The Kid heard the footsteps and whirled, proving that despite his show of indifference how alert he must have been.

'Hallo, Kid,' said Lobo.

The Kid did not answer but just stood looking at Lobo and slowly his thin lips began to curl.

'When you've finished your drink I want you to come down to the jail with me,' Lobo said. 'My pardner and I have a few more questions we'd like to ask you.'

'I'm thirsty,' said the Kid. 'I aim to have a lot of drinks.'

'I can't wait,' said Lobo. 'Just one — then we'll move. huh? Perhaps I didn't make myself clear. I'm taking you in again, Kid.'

'You can't get away with that. On what charge?'

'Like I said — more questions.' The Kid had emptied his glass. Lobo went on: 'Let's keep it friendly though, let you an' me have just one drink together before we go, huh?' He jerked his head. 'Set 'em up.'

The barman set them up. The Kid almost turned his back on Lobo again as, with his left hand, he reached for his second drink. Then, when he turned again, he had his gun in his right hand and it was pointed at Lobo's belly.

11

Lobo looked death in the face. Then Kid Moonlight began to back away from the bar and Lobo realized the young gunman didn't mean to shoot unless he had to. After all, Lobo did wear the talisman, the tin star.

Lobo knew he could not beat the Kid's trigger. The Kid looked like a cornered rat but he wasn't scared, he had just been pushed a little too far that was all. Maybe it was just his pride that was hurt. Lobo realized that if he made a false move the Kid would start blasting.

'Don't be a fool,' said Lobo.

'Put your hands on top of your head,' snarled the Kid. 'Go on, do as I say.'

Lobo raised his arms, placed his hands atop of his slouch hat. He felt kind of foolish, kind of mad; he forced himself to stay ice-cold, watching Kid

Moonlight like a hawk waiting to pounce.

The Kid continued to back. 'I've had enough,' he said. 'I'm getting out of here. Stay like that or, by Gar, I'll start shooting — an' I don't miss.'

He was almost at the batwings when a voice to the right of him said, 'Drop the gun, Kid.'

The Kid whirled, snapped a shot at Bruno Jensen in the corner. Bruno fired almost at the same instant. Both slugs missed their targets and did minor damage elsewhere. The Kid dived for the batwings, went through them almost headfirst. Lobo, gun drawn now, found there was nothing to shoot at. Bruno, smoking gun in fist, starting after the Kid, tripped over a chair and came down with a crash.

Lobo thought his sidekick had been hit. He ran over. Bruno, white and shaken, was climbing to his feet. He was still weak after his illness; shaken up, he discovered now that he wasn't half as tough as he had thought.

'You all right?'

'Sure, I'm all right,' said Bruno savagely. 'I just slipped, that was all.'

'Clumsy!' snapped Lobo. 'I'm going after that skunk. You stay right here, y'understand?'

'All right, boss,' said Bruno sullenly. He let himself fall into the chair.

The sound of hoofbeats was fading in the distance. The Kid had a start. Lobo ran outside. He hadn't got his own horse out this morning. He borrowed somebody else's, a rangy paint pony that looked fast. He didn't hear its owner yell after him as he thundered down the street.

When Lobo reached the end of the main drag, Kid Moonlight was just a cloud of dust out on the trail. A cloud of dust that veered off the trail as the Kid set off across country. In that direction lay the hills. Kid Moonlight was well-named: a night-rider, his horse was fleet, as precious to him and as well-tended as his guns. The Kid was making for the hills and the horse knew the hills well.

' Lobo Watkins guided his mount off the hard-packed trail too, on to the less even surface of bumps and ruts and hidden gopher-holes. The grass swished against the horse's legs. Lobo realized he had picked a little beauty: the paint pony was fast and sure-footed. It seemed to take to its new rider, give him all it had got.

There was no rain now and as the time was round about noon the sun was strong. Lobo became sticky with sweat. He pushed the horse on and the little beast respondled nobly. The miles fled by beneath his fleet hoofs. The sun was brassy and they were riding against it, so that Lobo had to pause from time to time to pick up sight of the Kid once more, a bobbing dot in the shimmering haze. Lobo began to wish that the rainy season didn't have these sudden changes, that the rain which he had cursed over the last few days, would start up again.

He did not get his wish. If anything the sun became even fiercer, a brassy gong vibrating in the sky, mocking him. The Kid had a mighty fast horse. He seemed to be drawing away. At times he was invisible, coming and going like a mirage.

The terrain was becoming even more uneven, rising; the foothills rose up out of the heat-haze and Lobo saw the Kid again climbing steadily.

'Come on, *chiquita*,' Lobo urged, driving his heels into the horse's flank.

The little beast quivered with power, tried . . . tried . . .

Kid Moonlight disappeared in the foothills.

A few seconds later the whiplash crack of a rifle sounded, awakening echoes. Something like an angry hornet buzzed near Lobo. He swerved the horse, reaching down instinctively for the saddle scabbard. There was no scabbard, no rifle. He realized then that he wasn't riding his own horse and he didn't have a rifle, only a Colt .45, hopeless at this range. He couldn't even see the Kid. But now a puff of smoke betokened the Kid's presence in the rocks.

This time the slug came nearer. The paint pony shied violently.

'Easy,' said Lobo. He left the saddle and began to run in a zig-zag, his gun in his hand now.

He threw himself flat on his belly. Another slug tugged at his hat but did not take it off. Lobo had fixed the Kid's position. He saw a movement, steel glinted. Lobo fanned the hammer of his gun, sending a stream of lead up there, pinning the Kid down, then he began to run again.

He reached the shelter of a small rock outcrop before the rifle bullets began to try and pick him out again. The Kid was evidently still in one piece.

The sun beat down on the top of Lobo's head. It flashed in his eyes when he looked up, seeking his opponent out. The rifle snarled again. A chip of rock bit savagely into Lobo's cheek, drawing blood. Lobo essayed another snap shot, shooting at the sun. Then he stopped to reload.

Kid Moonlight had everything, it seemed, on his side. He was higher up, had better cover and the sun at his back. He also had a rifle against Lobo's pistol.

Lobo could think of only one advantage, if any, that he had and maybe with this he was just being cocky. He was a mite older than the Kid and had probably seen a lot more action than that owl-hooter, daylight action, action in the sun and the rain along the border with the Legion, down South with the rebel army, in the streets of tough towns all over the West. He was a practised fighter: he had to think of some way to gain more advantage, to cut down the difference between the gun and the rifle.

If he could get the Kid rattled; if he could get behind him, or over top of him. If he could jump him somehow he wanted, if possible, to take him alive.

He took off his hat. He twisted his head, spotted a knob of rock which lay at the extreme end of the outcrop. He rose to one knee, keeping his head in cover. He tossed the hat towards the knob of rock. It lodged neatly, only to be blown off its perch again almost immediately. Lobo dived in the other direction.

He hit the ground, rolling. A slug chipped his heel. Kid Moonlight was a shooting fool. Crouching, bobbing, weaving, Lobo ran. A searing pain burned his thigh. He went flat. Stones bit into his hands and legs. But he realized he was in cover again. Just a bank of shale, safe as long as he didn't raise his head. He twisted his head, inspected his thigh. His trouser-leg was split open, a slug had creased his flesh, blood seeped sluggishly. But it wasn't bad.

He inspected the lie of the land. The Kid was silent, waiting for him to pop up like a turkey at a shoot.

Although Lobo's cover wasn't good

he had improved his position a little. Leastways, it was better as regards his proximity to his opponent. On the other hand, he had lost his hat, and the fierce rays of the sun beat down on his unprotected head.

He had an idea, however, that the Kid wasn't quite so well protected from him now: if Lobo made another dash in the same direction he might be able to outflank his opponent. That is, if he didn't get killed in the attempt. He wriggled forward a little, raised his head. A slug nearly took his ear off. He snapped a shot in return, in the direction of the blur of movement, the glint of steel which was Kid Moonlight.

Sweat began to run in rivulets down Lobo's face. If he didn't pass out with sunstroke he could play a waiting game. He had done it before. But the odds were still on his opponent's side. So he waited, while from time to time every time he moved, the Kid snapped a shot at him, pinning him down like a butterfly on a cork, using both rifle and revolver. The Kid was on a hair-trigger; Lobo hoped he was getting rattled.

He snapped shots at the Kid when he had a chance. But the Kid was still firmly entrenched and Lobo decided presently it was better to take another chance, make another bid, than crouch here like a crippled grasshopper and slowly frizzle to death.

He grabbed a handful of pebbles and threw them wildly, launched his body in the other direction. The lash of the rifle almost drowned the clatter of the pebbles. Lobo jarred his elbow on a rock. Then he was in cover again. He rose, gun ready. He saw the Kid's contorted face, the gleam of the rifle-barrel beneath it. The two men fired simultaneously. They both missed. They hugged cover.

Lobo, reloading swiftly, heard the Kid scrabbling around as he entrenched himself a little deeper. The sun was like a ball of molten copper, its rays like red-hot needles boring their way into Lobo's brain.

Dimly he heard the hoofbeats. He cocked his head on one side. The sound became quickly louder. The Kid shooting again, but this time his slugs came nowhere near Lobo.

Lobo rose to his feet. 'Kid!' he screamed. It was a terrifying sound, like the shriek of a blood-crazed savage.

Kid's face came into view; the staring eyes, the levelled rifle.

Half-crouching, Lobo fanned the hammer of his gun, sending a blistering hail of lead into the nest the other man had made for himself.

The rifle clattered on the rocks, steel winking derisively in the sun. Kid Moonlight rose to his full height, hands raised, talons clawing the brassy skies. He screamed once in agony, then pitched forward on his face. He lay still, spreadeagled across the rocks.

Lobo knew death when he saw it. He was kind of sorry. Kid Moonlight might have proved more valuable alive. Lobo felt flat; he wanted to sling his gun into the sky and turn away and walk, just walk.

But Bruno Jensen led his own horse and the little paint forward and Lobo went to meet him.

Bruno carried Lobo's hat too, his finger through the neat hole in the crown. 'I thought I'd come out an' see what was cookin',' he drawled. 'Lucky I heard the shootin' or I might've got lost.'

'Yeh, you might've got your head drilled too,' said Lobo. 'But thanks, anyway.'

'Yeh,' said Bruno. 'Looks like you got yourself another deputy, boss.'

Lobo grinned mirthlessly. 'Yeh, looks like it. Help me to get this carcass on the front of my saddle.'

They got back to Cravett in the somnolent late afternoon. The sun, half-obscured by a humid haze, was like a gout of putrid blood. The heat was oppressive.

'We'll have a hell of a storm anytime now,' muttered Lobo.

He felt flat, drained out. He had killed men before — many people had called him 'killer' — but it was never pleasant. What had he gained by killing Kid Moonlight? Even though it had had to be one or the other of them. If anything, he was further back now than when he started. Leastways he felt that way.

Maybe the weather had something to do with it. He didn't think he had ever seen a town so damp, clammily humid as Cravett. The evil which brooded over the town seemed to have an effect on the weather too. He shook his head violently, as if to shake himself free of his thoughts. He wasn't actually a fanciful man. But there was something about this hell-hole of a town.

Watching his silent saddle-pard out of the corner of his eye, Bruno Jensen wasn't particularly overjoyed by what he saw. He had seen Lobo in one of these moods before. Trouble was brewing up for somebody. Bad trouble. Bruno reminded himself that he could've been out of it all by now if he had obeyed orders. But he had elected to stick by 'the boss' and he meant to do so, even if he, the original 'Worst Shot in the West', got himself killed in the process.

The rutted main drag was empty and cracking in the sun. But now as the two riders with the grim burden across the saddle of one of the horses, drew nearer to the more popular area of town, loungers began to appear from the shadows like gophers from their holes.

The hanging body of Kid Moonlight no longer left a trail of blood in its wake. The Kid might have been no more than a swathe of crumpled rags flung over the front of Lobo's saddle, but the Kid had lost his hat and his lank black Indian hair hung down like a mourning banner, betokening that this shell had once been a man.

People didn't accost the two grim horsemen but only stood on the edges of the boardwalk while the name was whispered along. Then Lobo and Bruno stopped at the undertaking parlour and took the body inside, only to reappear again and finally incarcerate themselves in the sheriff's office.

Once the lawman and his saddle-pard were out of sight, a small crowd began to collect outside the undertaking parlour. Somebody found Duke Roland and aquainted him with the news and Duke came along and entered the undertaking establishment. He was in there about ten minutes. Then he reappeared and, looking neither to right or left, went purposefully down the street, in the opposite direction to the sheriff's office. Nobody followed him. Everybody knew better.

He was spotted going into the office of Lawyer Isaac Rooke and when he appeared again, retracing his steps, he had the little dried-up lawyer with him.

They went into the undertaking parlour, came out again, walked on, entered the sheriff's office.

Mike Daventry was in his swivel-chair behind the desk. Lobo and Bruno sat on the couch against the wall and quenched their thirsts in cold root beer.

Mike Daventry asked, 'What can I do for you, gentlemen?' He was nonchalant, he sounded perfectly sure of himself.

Duke Roland said, 'We've just been looking at the body of my friend, poor young Kid Moonlight. He's riddled with bullets, he never had a chance.'

There was a sound as if of smothered laughter. Duke glanced suspiciously at Bruno Jensen. Bruno, red in the face, began to cough. He waved the can of root beer. 'Went down the wrong way,' he explained.

'I was just about to go down and have a look at the Kid myself,' said Mike Daventry. 'Purely an official look, of course. The Kid was never a pretty specimen alive, so I doubt if he looks any better dead. He's no loss to the community, he had it coming to him. Poor young devil — I guess he was led astray by older folks. It does happen y'know . . . '

Throughout Mike's peroration Duke had been getting visibly more impatient. Now he glared at Lawyer Rooke and the little man took his cue and as Mike paused, put in his own two cents.

'Such levity is unbecoming to the law. It is just what one might expect, however, from a so-called peace-officer who hires a professional killer to do his dirty work for him.'

Bruno nudged his companion in the ribs. 'Hey, Lobo, the little freak's talkin' about you.'

'Is he now?' said Lobo and rose, advancing slowly on the little lawyer.

Isaac Rooke backed towards the door. 'You see,' he squeaked. 'Brutality — that's all you know . . . ' He dried up, mouthing, fishlike.

'Leave this to me, Lobo,' said Mike Daventry imperiously.

'Yes, sheriff,' said Lobo meekly and sat down again.

'The townsfolk won't lie down under this outrage,' said Duke Roland. 'Kid Moonlight was young and well-liked.

He was slaughtered like a cur.'

Lawyer Rooke had his cue again. With one eye warily on Lobo he said, 'Mr Roland approached me in the proper way, asking me to investigate this terrible thing. We came here in all humility, but determined to see justice done. It seems to me that of the people in this room, my client and I are the only two genuine representatives of justice. That man ... ' Isaac half-turned, raised his hand as if he would point an accusing finger at Lobo Watkins. But he met the cold sardonic gaze of the notorious killer's eye and he let the hand fall with a little slap to his side.

But he completed his sentence. 'That man should be indicted immediately for the murder of poor Kid Moonlight.'

'That's a laugh,' said Bruno Jensen.

'He certainly can spout, that leetle coyote,' said Lobo Watkins to nobody in particular. He was getting his spirits back. He was beginning to enjoy this.

Mike Daventry raised his hand. He

did manage to point an accusing finger — right at the shyster lawyer.

Then, brooking no interruptions now, he told the story just the way it had happened. The Kid had pulled a gun on Lobo: the barman at Sadie's place would back that. And — the finality — Lobo had killed the Kid in self-defence, his gun against the other's rifle. And Bruno Jensen was right here to back that up — which he did.

'A trumped-up story,' said Lawyer Rooke. 'Believe me, gentlemen, you won't hear the last of this.'

'Is that a threat?' demanded the sheriff.

But the lawyer was turning to Duke and with great dignity, without a parting word, the big-shot gambler led the way out.

After a moment Mike Daventry said, 'So Duke's turned over a new leaf, so now he's a law-abiding citizen with a sense of outraged indignation. You got to hand it to the man — he's as cunning as a wagon-load of monkeys.'

12

The evening was a quiet one. Maybe the rough element, with the terrible example before them of the bullet-riddled carcass of Kid Moonlight, were minding their Ps and Qs. On the other hand, maybe they were following Duke's lead and acting for once like exemplary citizens.

They bided their time. They sweated and chatted. But there was less raucous noise than usual; an almost brooding stillness hung over the town. Then, with nightfall, thunder crashed and the storm broke. In a matter of moments the main drag was a river of mud.

Tired and hungry after their long ride, Lobo and Bruno partook of a man-sized meal in Sadie's place. People ran in like half-drowned rats, skirted the table where the two men sat, shot covert glances in that direction.

Nobody spoke to them: even the ordinary, ostensibly-honest townsfolk seemed reluctant to do so. The place became filled to suffocation as people used the rain as an excuse for an early night on the drink.

Mike Daventry came in and joined his two friends. Duke Roland, strangely enough, was not in evidence. Maybe he was still mourning the death of his 'poor young friend' Kid Moonlight.

The three friends raked in Pegleg Brown, and the quartet — complete with bottle, glasses and plenty of smokes — adjourned to Bruno's room for a game of poker. And so, while the storm raged outside, the night passed.

The next morning people wallowed around in treacly black mud while rain drizzled miserably from lowering skies.

The sheriff and Lobo had decided to ride out to the Craddock ranch. Bruno had dealt himself in and Lobo was resigned to this. So after breakfast, the three of them, suitably clad, set off.

As the visitors rode past the corral,

men came from the ranch buildings to meet them.

'Now take it easy, you two,' Mike Daventry cautioned his two friends.

George Pinfold hollered, 'Light down, gents. C'mon into the dry.'

The visitors dismounted awkwardly with flapping slickers. A couple of men came forward to take their horses. The law sloshed forward with beanpole George dancing attendance and entered the bunkhouse. Men were already there, almost as if waiting. More men trooped in behind the visitors.

' 'Tain't fit for a dawg to be out,' said George Pinfold affably. 'Set, gents . . . ' He raised his voice to a bellow. 'Porky! Cawfee!'

The fat cook bustled from the kitchen with a tray full of large, thick steaming mugs of hot coffee. The three visitors divested themselves of their slickers and hats — but not their gunbelts — and quaffed the powerful liquid gratefully.

All around them men were swigging

noisily. But nobody else seemed to be sitting down.

After a moment, George Pinfold said, 'Allus glad to welcome old friends. Excuse me asking though, gents, but did you come out here for any particular reason?'

'We didn't ride all this way jest for our health,' retorted Lobo Watkins.

Mike Daventry nudged him, then looking the Craddock ramrod straight in the eye, said 'That was a fool stunt you pulled the other night, George.'

George Pinfold raised his eyebrows. He wasn't used to such plain shooting from the aged sheriff of Cravett.

'You think so?' he said. 'Well, it got us no place after all did it? Just one good man dead, that was all.'

'Amos Moon,' snapped Lobo Watkins. 'What was good about *him*?'

Lobo didn't like all these tough monkeys standing round him, looking down at him. He was about to rise when Mike Daventry caught his arm.

'By the way, George,' said Mike. 'I

don't think you've met our friend here.'

'No, I guess not.' There was a sardonic note in George's voice. 'I was rude. I should've waited for a formal introduction.'

'This is Bruno Jensen, Cal's brother.'

George's manner changed. 'Well!' He stuck out his hand. 'Cal was my pard. We all miss him. That was quite a play you made for Clay Bogaine, pardner, I heard about it.'

Bruno, his hand caught in a vice-like grip, said ruefully, 'I stuck out my neck there all right.'

'It took guts to walk into that hornets' nest on your lonesome an' make your play,' George Pinfold said. 'I heard you took care of another skunk yesterday too — Kid Moonlight.'

'News sure travels fast,' said Lobo Watkins.

Bruno Jensen said, 'That was Lobo's play, Mr Pinfold. I just happened along. Boy, you should've seen the way Lobo cut that coyote down.'

'Yeh,' said George flatly. 'Your friend

Lobo is quite a bobcat, ain't he?'

'I try to do my two-cents' worth, Mr Pinfold,' put in Lobo.

'We all do, Mr Watkins,' said George softly.

Sheriff Daventry put in quickly, 'Mr Jensen has been wanting to see you an' thank you for what your boys tried to do for his brother.'

'We tried to save him,' said George, 'but we were too late.'

Others of the Craddock men had crowded nearer. Some of them shook Bruno by the hand. His hell-raising brother, Cal, had been a popular cuss.

Only the new riders hung back, tough, watchful. But they were outnumbered. The tension was relaxed a little.

Mike Daventry said, 'We've got a couple of your boys in jail, George. A couple of new boys, I think.'

'Yes, that is so,' said George. 'I'm glad you reminded me about that. I didn't know anything about those four boys sticking up the jail until I heard about it afterwards. It was Amos

Moon's idea. I — er — um — apologize for any inconvenience that was caused to you and your — um — deputy.'

'Granted,' said Sheriff Daventry quickly. 'We'll let those two boys loose when we get back, George. We've told them they must leave the territory. We hope you'll co-operate — if they come here, pay 'em off an' speed them on their way.'

'I'll do that, sheriff.'

Lobo was tired of all this fancy talk. 'While you're about it,' he said harshly, 'there are three other skunks here you can speed on their way too. They were in the jail stick-up.'

As Lobo well knew, for he had spotted them, the three men were right there in the bunkhouse. One of them started forward. Lobo began to rise. Pinfold turned his head, flapped a hand. The truculent hardcase let himself fall back to a sitting position on a bunk.

Pinfold turned to Lobo again. 'You're a very arrogant man, Mr Watkins,' he said softly.

'Am I?' Lobo waited.

George Pinfold's manner changed again. 'Coffee?' he asked of nobody in particular. He raised his voice and bellowed again and the fat cook appeared with steaming refills.

'I've got some'n to show you, sheriff,' said George. 'I'll go fetch it.' He left the bunkhouse.

Bruno was exchanging anecdotes about his late brother with men who had known Cal Jensen, rode with him, drunk with him, helped him to raise hell. Mike Daventry seemed to have sunk into a brown study. The disgruntled hardcases glowered in the background, the newly-hired trouble-shooters: Lobo kept a wary eye on them through the steam as he sipped the strong fragrant coffee.

George Pinfold returned. On to the long bunkhouse table he tossed a silk kerchief. It was a little muddy but the pattern was clearly discernible. The background was a rich chocolate brown and on this were printed decorations in the form of red, white and blue flags, tiny stars and stripes.

'That's mighty patriotic,' said Bruno Jensen.

The three visitors took the kerchief one by one and inspected it. It was of fine shot silk and, despite the mud, all in one piece. Pretty new, too.

'One of the men found it,' said George Pinfold. 'On the edge of the little valley where those four night-raiders were murdered and the cattle run off. It'd been trampled in the ground, that's why we didn't notice it before, I guess.'

'Who found it?' asked Lobo Watkins suspiciously.

'Brinny Capes found it.'

A tubby little cowhand stepped forward. 'Howdy, Brinny,' said Mike Daventry.

George Pinfold said, 'Brinny's been riding for this ranch for five years.'

Lobo Watkins decided there was no guile in that moon face, that tubby puppyish body.

'None of our boys've claimed it,' said

George. 'It must've belonged to one o' those murdering rustlers.'

'It's the first clue we've had,' said Mike Daventry. He tucked the kerchief carefully into the top pocket of his shirt and buttoned the flap. He rose. 'I'll guess we'll ride,' he said. 'Thanks for the sustenance.'

Their horses, dried and fed, were brought for them. They set off back through the drizzle.

After a bit, Mike Daventry said, 'Well, I don't think that was a wasted journey anyway.'

Lobo said: 'D'yuh think you an' me would've got out of there all in one piece if Bruno hadn't been with us.'

'Aw, Lobo, George Pinfold ain't that bad. I figure he'll play along with us.'

'A decent bunch of hombres,' was Bruno's contribution.

Lobo snorted. 'I pass,' he said, and bent his head against the rain.

They got back in time for the funeral of Kid Moonlight, though they took no part in it.

The 'underworld' of Cravett had turned up in force, and a more decorous band of underworld characters would have been hard to find. Not to be outdone by the mourners of Jake Morgan, Kid Moonlight's confraternities had fixed up a real old Western funeral for their boy too.

The bearers, with Duke Roland head and shoulders above the others, were all in black. Duke would have done credit to a Fifth Avenue tailor. In the drizzling rain and the black mud the cortège trudged up Boot Hill. Preacher Holmes had been conscripted. The world wept from lowering brows. The Preacher did Kid Moonlight proud. There were flowers, too.

The three returned wayfarers had a hot meal, then sought out Sadie Cane and showed her the fancy kerchief.

At first she shook her head. Then she said, 'Wait a minute. I have seen it before. I was trying to think of a man wearing it, that was what foxed me. It was a woman I saw wearing it. In fact, it was one of my own girls.'

'Get her!'

It was Pegleg Brown who got her finally. She proved to be a petite, dark Mexican girl called Estrallita. Her eyes were like brown pools, flashing and rippling at the men who surrounded her. But these *hombres* were impervious to her charms. They just wanted to know something.

Sadie spoke then, 'Estrallita, do you remember the beautiful brown silk kerchief of yours I admired some time ago? The one with the tiny red, white and blue flags on it.'

Estrallita wrinkled her nose pertly. Then her eyes widened. 'Ah, but yes.'

'What happened to it?'

She pouted. 'A man stole it. He promised to give eet back. But he did not.'

'Is this the kerchief?' Sadie produced it.

The girl grabbed it. 'But yes. But eet is all muddy! How did you get eet? Where . . . '

'More of that later. Tell me, Estrallita — this is very important — who was the man who stole it from you?'

'A big yellow-haired man with funny teeth. Like thees.' Estrallita made a grimace, showed her white molars in a buck-toothed snarl; then she went into peals of laughter.

Nobody else laughed. They all looked at her intently. Estrallita dried up, her eyes wider than ever. 'Do you know the man's name?' asked Sadie.

'Yes, I think they call him Rabbit. His face is like that.' Estrallita started to grimace again, then thought better of it. 'But hee's not a rabbit. He ees big and tough. A brute. Faugh!'

The men looked at Sadie. She shook her head. 'Probably one of the hard boys who hung around Duke Roland. They come an' go.'

'Yes, I have seen heem with Duke,' put in Estrallita.

'Have you seen him recently?'

'Yes.' I saw heem the other night. I do not speak to heem — he frightens me.'

'Look for him tonight,' said Sadie. 'And if you see him tell me.'

'I weell.'

'Not a word to anybody else about this. Not even to one of the other girls, you understand. Not a word!'

Estrallita looked around her at the grim faces. 'I weell not talk,' she said. 'I promise. And I weell tell you if I see heem. He ees a pig.'

Waggling her trim hips, she left the room.

Lobo and Mike went back to the jail. They let loose the two ex-Craddock cases and told them to hit the trail for places unknown. The two battered men promised to do so. They sounded as if they meant it too.

Lobo went around to the livery-stables to see Jake. The red-bearded man was sleeping. He was doing a lot of that. Doc said not to bother Jake: if he had anything to tell, he'd tell it when he was good and ready.

Night fell. The honky-tonks started to light up, let loose their noise, their cajolement. Lobo and Mike went to

Sadie's place again, joined Bruno. They watched Estrallita, watched Sadie, but there was no sign from either of them. When Sadie had a chance to approach them she did so, but she had no news.

The night was pretty much the same as usual. Kid Moonlight's erstwhile mourners seemed already to have forgotten their 'poor young friend'. Duke Roland held court in his usual corner. The band played. Couples shuffled in travesties of the dance. The chips clicked; the wheels chirruped; the croupiers intoned the odds. The rain still drizzled outside but, after the storm that had preceded it, it was hardly noticeable.

The night passed and the man called Rabbit did not put in an appearance.

Bruno went upstairs to join Lucinda. The saloon was almost empty. Finally, Lobo and Mike said 'Goodnight' to Sadie and went out into the darkness.

13

The rain drizzled miserably. The night was black. Lights were going out one by one. There was nothing in the immediate vicinity except the pale yellow effusion from Sadie's place. A gun boomed. Mike Daventry gave a little grunt and went back against the wall. Lobo dropped on one knee, his gun out. A slug whined over his head and thunked into the batwings behind him. He fired at the yellow flash on the other side of the road. He twisted his head.

'Mike?'

'I'm all right,' gasped the sheriff. 'The light! Get out of the light. The skunks, they . . . '

More shooting drowned the rest of his sentence. Glass shattered in one of the saloon windows. Lobo flung himself sideways into the meagre shelter of a post of the hitching-rail. He heard Mike scrambling along behind him. He snapped another couple of shots to the other side of the street. A slug bit into wood. Chips stung his cheeks. Mike rolled on his belly beside him.

'C'mon!' Lobo made another dive, reached the shelter of a cast-iron horse-trough. Mike was shooting now, grunting as he again joined Lobo. A regular barrage was set up from over the way.

Slugs pinged into the metal horse-trough, ricocheted, whined away into the darkness. Echoes rolled in the still moments. The fighting gunmen had the street to themselves in the rain and mud: if anybody else had been around, they had quickly made themselves scarce.

'You hurt?' asked Lobo.

'Jest creased my left shoulder. Nothin' to worry about. Who are the skunks, I wonder. How many?'

'Two — three — maybe more. Hasty though. They could've got us both out there in the light if they had taken their time about it.'

A vague shape flittered on the other side of the main drag. Both Lobo and Mike snapped shots at it, but did not know whether they had scored a mark. The bushwhackers opened up again in force. Gunfire made the night hideous. Mike cursed as a slug took his hat off.

The two men kept their heads down. Lobo was flat on his belly now, firing around the end of the horse-trough.

He called: 'Where're they holed-up?'

'There's another trough like this one on the other side of the road,' said Mike. 'Remember? Also, close to that, there is a big old iron-rimmed wagon-wheel on the sidewalk propped up to advertise the cantina called The Wagon Wheel.'

'Oh, yeh — yeh.' Gunfire, slugs humming perilously close, made further conversation impossible.

Mike heard Lobo yell 'If we could only . . . '

A barrage of shots drowned everything out. The two lawmen retaliated fiercely.

There was a lull. Then the shooting broke out again but, strangely enough, no slugs seemed to be coming near the two lawmen now.

'What the heck!' said Lobo.

'Maybe it's Sadie an' Bruno an' Pegleg. Maybe . . . '

'What! From out there?'

The shooting was going crazy on the other side of the road. Yellow spurts of flame blazoned in all directions. It almost looked as if the bushwhackers were fighting among themselves. A man screamed in awful agony. The sound died away in a gurgle.

Then suddenly it was all over except the echoes.

Then a voice yelled, 'Daventry! Watkins! We're coming over.' And down the street hoofbeats started up frantically, dying quickly away in the night.

'That's George Pinfold's voice,' said Mike Daventry.

He yelled: 'All right, c'mon over. Take it easy.'

Across the river of mud the two

figures appeared, slowly taking concrete shape. The two lawmen, guns cocked, watched them until they reached the sideway, until they saw the two newcomers, long and lean and short and tubby, swing their hands laxly at their sides, well away from their weapons.

Lights were going on along the street. Sadie Cane ran from the saloon, behind her Bruno, Pegleg and Lucinda. They all carried weapons. Even Lucinda was toting a heavy Colt.

'It's all over bar the cheering,' called George Pinfold cheerily.

'Gosh, George, I nearly shot you,' cried Sadie. 'What's goin' on? Who . . . is anybody hurt?'

'Nobody this side o' the street I don't think,' said George. 'At least, we're all standin' upright.'

'Mike got creased on the shoulder,' said Lobo. 'I ain't been touched.' He was looking at Pinfold's stocky companion. Finally he recognized the plump moonfaced Craddock hand who had found the flag-decorated kerchief out on the range. The man called Brinny Capes. The man Lobo had thought to be a puppyish simpleton.

George Pinfold spoke up again, soberly now. 'It was those three skunks I gave marching orders to this afternoon. The three men who were concerned in the jail hold-up. Brinny here was on night duty. He spotted 'em riding in the direction of town, instead of the opposite way like I had told 'em. I had a hunch they might be trying to get even with the law of Cravett — so me an' Brinny came a-riding.'

Lobo reflected that Brinny was certainly the little man who kept his eyes peeled. First the kerchief, and now this.

Mike Daventry said: 'We're certainly obliged to you both.'

Brinny Capes said nothing but he seemed to be smiling plumply.

George Pinfold said: 'We got two of 'em. Brinny got one an' I got the other. They're both dead. The other one got away. I guess we won't be seeing *him* again.'

Lights shone out on to the street, making the mud like black oil. Now the shooting had finished, people were coming out of their holes. Somebody had found the two bodies on the opposite sidewalk and loud speculation was going on.

'We better go over there,' said Lobo. The group began to move. Lobo fell into step beside George Pinfold. Lobo said:

'So you did what I asked an' sent those three galoots packing?'

'I did! Did you think I wouldn't?'

George didn't wait for an answer, but went on: 'In our separate ways, Mr Watkins — or may I call you Lobo? — you and I are on the same side. I always aim to co-operate with the law, except when the law ain't above-board, of course.'

'It's above-board now, George,' said Lobo.

'Yeh, I guess it is.'

'An' the law's mighty obliged for the help of you an' your pard.'

'You can count on Brinny,' said George, 'and any of the rest of my boys.'

Lobo had nothing to say to this and — as if divining his companion's thoughts — the Craddock ramrod went on, asked a question: 'You don't think it was a good idea bringing in gunnies from outside?'

'Maybe — maybe not. I guess you figured to fight fire with fire. Cain't really blame you for that.'

'Are there any more of those boys you particularly object to?'

'Amos Moon was the only one I recognized — an' Amos ain't gonna bother anybody any more.'

'Uh — well — maybe I'll sort 'em over again.'

They had reached the people gathered around the bodies. There were two groups actually, for the bodies were apart. One of the men looked as if he had been running for it when he was

215

hit. He had stopped a slug on the side of his head. His pard had head and shoulders through the spokes of the huge wagon-wheel and hung there like a sacrifice. He was stitched up the middle and had died with a terrible look of agony on his face.

'More work for the undertaker,' said Brinny Capes.

As far as Lobo could remember those were the only words the little moon-faced cowhand spoke that night.

* * *

Lobo Watkins didn't have a particularly suspicious nature. He had the inherent caution and cold hair-trigger nerves of the gunfighter; plus a fiery temper, which he, however, could hold in check when need be. He owed his life many times over to his caution, his ability to assert his will over his temper: a gunfighter couldn't afford to go off half-cocked. Still and all, despite his experience of treachery, cunning and greed (to his mind the ingredients of all badness) he did not think he was over-suspicious of his fellow-men.

Nevertheless, there was something about this town, this hell-hole called Cravett, that made him mistrust everybody except those persons closest to him.

Although George Pinfold and Brinny Capes had saved Lobo and Mike's bacon last night, Lobo still couldn't make up his mind whether the Craddock men were genuine or not.

Had George spoken the truth when he said Amos Moon had been responsible for the jail hold-up? Amos wasn't here to dispute the fact and the tale seemed a bit thin anyway. Could be, though.

Had George and Brinny really tailed the three bush-whackers like they claimed because they figured the lawmen were in danger? Or had they ridden into town and taken care of the men in order to shut their mouths for good: a custom that seemed to be mighty popular around these parts? Lobo was in a kind of a tangle. So he gave George and his buddies the benefit of the doubt. For the time being, anyway.

By daylight the rain had finally let up again. A pale sickly sun shone on the river of mud that was the main drag. In the worst spots planks and duckboards had been thrown across from sidewalk to sidewalk so that people could go about their business without actually wallowing in the slime which, where it wasn't black and oily, was red and cloying.

Staid businessmen tried to look as dignified as possible as they walked the plank. The younger section of the community amused themselves by playing last across, or fighting on the bridges and howling with glee when one of them was precipitated into the slime. Loungers whistled and yippee'ed as percentage girls going about their shopping showed more leg than was customary as they negotiated the boards. In the honky-tonks at night these fillies were expected to show as much leg as possible, but by day, dressed in their frills and laces and bustles, they were mysterious again and, with the mud as a prime excuse, took delight in lifting a tiny corner of the veil and giving the men an early-morning treat.

The rain had long since washed the blood from the boardwalk outside The Wagon Wheel cantina, from the spokes and rims of the huge wagon wheel itself where one of the bushwhackers had hung and dripped like a side of beef. The two bodies lay in the undertaking parlour. They would be buried quickly in a short while.

Mike Daventry's shoulder had proved to be only a flesh wound, similar to the crease Lobo had got in his leg the day before when he fought and killed Kid Moonlight. Both the lawmen were still fighting fit. They were in the sheriff's office when the deputation called.

The deputation consisted of half-a-dozen of the regular townsmen. They were all in business in one way or another in Cravett itself and none of them was what might be called active members of the rough element. Lobo Watkins was of the opinion that they were a pretty shifty-looking bunch for all that. Their spokesman was a pot-bellied character in wrinkled brown store-clothes. He was introduced to Lobo as 'Repton' or 'Ripton' or something like that and he seemed very reluctant to shake the notorious killer's hand.

He took a long time to come to the point — if, indeed, he managed to come to the point at all. But the gist of his verbal perambulations was as follows:

Sheriff Mike Daventry had been sworn in as sheriff by the late lamented mayor of Cravett, Jake Priest. Jake — God rest his soul — had been a friend of every man here, except, of course, of Mr Watkins, who hadn't had the great fortune of knowing old Jake, a straight-shooting white man if ever there was one. Now there was no mayor and there should be a mayor and the deputation didn't think Sheriff Daventry had the right to swear in deputies, particularly outsiders: that should be the mayor's job. Hired gunmen (no names mentioned!) were no good, they killed too easily, there had been too much bloodshed. The deputation suggested that the sheriff get rid of his deputy (er — deputies!) until a new mayor was elected. There were nominations, it wouldn't take long to elect a mayor.

Had they anybody particular in mind?

We-ell . . .

Actually there had only been one nomination so far. A man of exemplary character.

That was how Duke Roland's name entered into the conversation. Strangely enough, neither the sheriff nor his sidekick seemed surprised at hearing that name crop up again. They were pretty non-committal about it, however; and then the deputation left.

'So our worthy model citizen has released another shaft,' said Lobo.

Mike sighed. 'Yeh, that was all pretty obvious, wasn't it? It's not generally known — except by the people directly concerned, of course — that Duke Roland owns quite a lot of property in this town. More things than mere money have changed hands over his gaming table. Those boys, if I remember 'em rightly, all occupy or do business in property owned by Duke. They sing to the Duke's tune. They are scared of being turned out or of having regrettable 'accidents' happen to them or members of their families . . . '

Mike's weather-wrinkled cheeks curled in a bitter smile. 'They take the line of least resistance. I should be the last one to condemn them for that — I guess I was doing the same thing myself until you came along.'

'Forget it,' snapped Lobo.

He touched the star at his breast. 'You don't want this!' It was more of a statement than a question.

'Not unless you want to give it to me,' said Mike.

'I guess I'll hang on to it a while longer, if it's all the same to you.'

Mike smiled again, more mirth in it now. 'I won't take it from you then — yet.'

'So we'll go on as before — an' see what happens. Chow at Sadie's now, huh?'

'Chow,' agreed Mike and led the way.

After breakfast with Mike, Bruno and Pegleg Brown, Lobo climbed the stairs to say good morning to Sadie.

Sadie stood in the passage outside the door of her opulent sitting-room. She was dressed to kill and was shaking the hand of a thickset, florid middle-aged character in swell clothes of Eastern cut. She saw Lobo and called him, introduced him to Mr Rafe Spalletti, a business man from Chicago.

Mr Spalletti had a gold watch-chain

that must've weighed a ton draped across his well-fed torso. He said he was pleased to meet Lobo and inspected him with shrewd little eyes. He had a grip like a bearcub.

He said he would get in touch with Miss Cane. Then, with a final bow, he took his leave.

'Best sitting-room too,' said Lobo with a grin. 'And all the frills and furbelows. What do we do now pore ol' Lobo's arrived — adjourn to the kitchen?'

'Not in this dress.'

'And what was all that intended for?'

'That will have to be a secret for a bit.'

'Like that, huh?'

Sadie gave him a coquettish look from her fine eyes. 'Jealous?'

'Should I be?'

'No. You never should be — you know that.' She linked her arm in his and led him into the sitting-room. But they were not to be left in opulent dalliance for long, for the door was rapped and Pegleg's voice hollered:

'Sadie! Estrallita's here. She wants to see you like crazy. She's hoppin' around like a cat on hot stones.'

Sadie and Lobo exchanged glances, rose. 'Send her in,' called Sadie.

Estrallita's dark eyes were enormous with excitement. 'He ees downstairs,' she cried. 'The peeg: the one they call Rabbit.'

Sadie purposely made light of it. 'Pig? Rabbit? How the child does run on! But you have done well, Estrallita. I will reward you later. Stay here. I will send for you if I want you.' She pointed. 'There are chocolates on the table there.'

'But, yes,' said Estrallita, and sat down as near to the chocolates as she could get. It was a great honour to be allowed to stay alone in Sadie's magnificent room.

'I'll handle this,' said Lobo.

'I'll be right behind you,' said Sadie. And indeed she was as they descended the stairs.

Rabbit lived up to his name. He was a big man but he had an evil ratlike face with very prominent rabbit-teeth. Mike and Bruno were one at each side of him at the bar. Evidently they had recognized him by the description Estrallita had given earlier.

Lobo nodded and Mike, knowing then that his surmise had been correct, stepped forward and confronted the man.

'I'd like you to take a pasear down to the office with me, son,' Mike drawled. 'I've got a few questions I'd like to ask you.'

Rabbit, surprised, all teeth now, turned towards Mike. Bruno stole up behind him and neatly lifted his gun from its holster. By that time Lobo had approached. Rabbit found himself ringed by three determined characters.

'What the hell does this mean? I . . . '

'Walk, son,' said Mike.

'You can't get away with this. I ain't done anything. I just . . . '

'The man said walk,' intoned Lobo.

Rabbit took one look at those cold deadly eyes and began to walk.

Bruno, who was not an official deputy yet, reluctantly stayed behind. Mike and Lobo took Rabbit down to the jail and locked him in a cell.

'Let him simmer for a while,' said Lobo. 'Maybe he'll talk all the better then.'

So they sat at the desk and played cards.

Rabbit yelled once. Lobo went down to the cell and told the prisoner that if he didn't shut his yap they'd turn the hose on him.

The lawmen decided to have a frugal lunch in the office and keep an eye on their prisoner. Lobo went to the door and called a passing kid and sent him down the street for some sandwiches, hot coffee and a modicum of rum.

The two men imbibed desultorily over their cards as the afternoon shadows lengthened. Mike had lost his abnormal craving for liquor. He could take it or leave it. He looked ten years younger than when Lobo saw him that first day. A few weeks ago, that was all, though at times to Lobo they indeed seemed like ten years.

Hell, it was beginning to rain again.

The prisoner wasn't supplied with any food or drink. Evidently, he hadn't the heart to yell for any. He was silent and when Lobo went to take a look at him, he merely scowled and spat on the floor between his feet like a sulky urchin.

The lawman had half-hoped another deputation would turn up, solely on poor Rabbit's behalf. Or maybe Duke and his pet lawyer Isaac Rooke. But nothing like that happened and the day got long in the tooth and they had to light the lamp.

'I figure you owe me about two thousand dollars,' said Mike.

'Yeh. As I remember, you allus were sharp with the cards.'

'Do tell! Mebbe I could've made my mark thataway and lived off the fat o' the land and been a fancy Dan like Duke Roland.'

'An' died young, no doubt. While look at yuh — the happy oldster. You're such an old mossy-horn you're beginning to get petrified.'

'Pickled's the word,' said Mike and took another swig of liquor.

'What's going on out there?' bellowed the prisoner suddenly. 'Can't I have some light?'

'He's found his voice,' said Mike.

'Maybe he's scared o' the dark.' Lobo rose. 'Whatsay I take that kerchief an' try an' get him to sing me a song about it?'

Mike produced the kerchief of chocolate-brown shot silk decorated with tiny red, white and blue flags. He handed it over. Lobo crumpled it into a ball in his brown fist, held it there as he went through into the cell-block, closing the door gently behind him.

Rabbit was cursing to himself. Lobo found a lucifer, scratched one, lit the hanging lantern which threw light into the cell. He stood looking through the barred door. Rabbit sat huddled on the bunk and scowled at him.

Lobo held his fist under the light and opened it and let the silk kerchief fall slowly apart, finally to dangle from his fingers.

He watched the man's eyes and saw them widen involuntarily, before Rabbit hid them beneath lowered lids.

'You've seen this before, ain't you?'

'No. What is it?'

'It's a kerchief. A fancy kerchief. Brown silk with decorations. Look, see the purty little flags.'

'It looks like a woman's scarf to me. What would I be doing with a woman's scarf? Are you tryin' to be funny?'

'Not particularly. You better take a good look at this scarf, as you call it, Rabbit. Look, it's kinda muddy. It looks like it's been trampled on. Do you still say you've never seen it before?'

'Yeh. I told yuh, didn't I?'

Lobo thrust the kerchief nearer to the bars. 'Take another good look at it. Just a kerchief — a scarf. But, unless you decide to sing us a tune, this is gonna hang you, I promise you that.'

Rabbit was silent, his head bent. 'Next time I come I'll have the keys with me,' said Lobo. 'I'll come in an' give you a much closer look at the scarf. You an' me will have a real heart-to-heart talk.'

Still no answer. Lobo left Rabbit to his thoughts.

He returned to the office just as a boy entered with some more eats and coffee. Lobo thoughtfully left the door of the cell-block open, so that Rabbit could get a whiff of the fragrant smell: what might be termed a 'high tea' of ham, beans, fried eggs sunny-side-up, hot cakes and syrup, rum and coffee.

Mike swept the cards aside. 'Two thousand, five hundred,' he said.

'I'll trade you this for it,' said Lobo. He took off his star and placed it on the desk. He jerked a thumb. 'I'm goin' in there later on to take that skunk apart.'

'So,' drawled Mike. 'Waal, I wouldn't

want you to get your badge dented.' He drew the star closer to him. 'So I'll keep it for you for a while.'

Lobo grinned, sat down and began to attack the eats.

Afterwards they smoked and played cards some more. Lobo kept on losing. But he was getting impatient — and not only with his cards. Finally, he rose and asked Mike for the keys. Mike handed them over silently and Lobo went into the cell-block, closing the door behind him.

In the feeble rays thrown into the cell by the hurricane-lantern, Rabbit sat straddle-legged with his big-knuckled hands hanging between his knees. He was a big ape-like man. He glowered at Lobo from under beetling brows and growled, 'If you ain't gonna let me go, jest leave me alone.'

He lowered his head again but there was a tenseness about him. Lobo smiled sardonically and unlocked the door. He opened it and stepped inside. He half-turned to close the door behind him and, like a cornered rat, the prisoner sprang.

Lobo whirled, brought up the key ring in his hand. The heavy bunch of keys caught Rabbit on the side of the face and he clapped his hand to the place and staggered back against the wall.

Blood oozed through his fingers. His eyes mirrored insane murder. 'I don't figure I need these really,' said Lobo and tossed the keys through the barred door and they clinked against the passage-wall.

Lobo was not wearing his gunbelt or hat. He was stripped for action.

Rabbit sprang again, blood streaming from his face, bright drops of it spattering Lobo with the violence of the attack. The man's mouth was open, his rabbit-teeth were the snarling teeth of an enraged animal. His hands reached for Lobo like talons, missing, scrabbling at Lobo's shirt. But there wasn't enough room to dodge and the two men closed awkwardly.

Lobo drove a fist low, felt it sink into the pulpy ring of his opponent's middle. The man grunted and spluttered. Lobo was a little nauseated as blood spattered his face. He struck out again but Rabbit was moving and the blow only got him on the shoulder, knocking him back on to the bunk. From there, as Lobo advanced, Rabbit lashed out with both feet.

The double-blow was not solid or Lobo might have been winded completely. As it was he was knocked back against the cell door with a force that shook every bone in his body. Rabbit, over-eager, his eyes blazing madly, charged after him. Lobo side-stepped and it was Rabbit's turn to run into the barred door, but head-on.

Rabbit staggered back, dazedly. Lobo chopped the man across the throat and once more Rabbit went back to the bunk, crouched there choking and spluttering.

A voice behind Lobo said: 'Why play

with him? Why waste your time?'

Lobo turned his head. Mike Daventry stood in the passage, the keys in one hand, a gun in the other. Lobo realized the gun was his own.

'Why waste time?' repeated Mike. 'Take this.' He pushed the gun through the bars.

Lobo took it. 'You're right,' he said.

He turned, stared at Rabbit. The big weasel-faced man was tough. He was bracing himself again but when he saw the gun he subsided and for the first time a look of fear came into his eyes.

'Yes, why should I waste my time an' my energy on a murderous cur like this one,' said Lobo half to himself.

Rabbit licked lips gone suddenly dry. Then Lobo was looking at him again, speaking directly to him.

'Have you ever been pistol-whipped, Rabbit? It ain't pretty. A man could die from it. But he'd go through hell before he died.'

'You're bluffing,' said Rabbit hoarsely. 'I ain't done nothing. The people would . . .'

'Remember the pretty scarf, Rabbit,' cut in Lobo. 'It was found out on the range right near to where the four Craddock night-riders were murdered. The murderers wore dark scarves over their faces.'

'You've got no proof that I was there. Somebody could've taken my scarf . . . '

'So you admit it was your scarf, the scarf that you stole from Estrallita, Sadie's Mexican girl?'

There was a sudden clatter in the passage. Half-turning his head, Lobo kept the gun covering Rabbit, watched him out of one eye. A newcomer had joined Mike Daventry. It was the little Mexican boy called, if Lobo remembered rightly, Manuel. He was the sidekick of Lopez of the livery-stables.

He shrilled: 'Señor Lobo, the big red one, Mad Jake, he wants to see you — *muy pronto.*'

'You better go, Lobo,' said Mike. 'It might be mighty important. I'll watch this skunk.'

'Yeh — yeh.'

Mike kept Rabbit covered while Lobo left the cell. 'Don't try anything foolish, old-timer. Let this skunk simmer till I come back.'

'Sure,' said Mike.

With his arm round the boy's shoulders, Lobo went out into the rain. He helped the boy along; they ran to the livery-stables.

14

Jake was sitting up in his bunk. His hair and beard had been combed, his eyes were clear again, a rational light in them.

Lopez was there but he joined the boy outside in the stables, leaving the two old friends together.

There was something of the old power in the grip of Jake's hand.

He said: 'The Doc tells me I've been half-crazy for some time, no hoax about it this time. He says it was as if I had somep'n on my mind that, for a long time, prevented me from getting well. There was something on my mind, I guess, Lobo. It would've stayed there and I should probably have cashed in my chips sooner or later if somehow — I don't know how, really, it was as if you spoke to me — I learned that you meant to stick by me no matter what. I gotta thank you most fervently for that old-timer.'

He waved his big hand, quelling anything Lobo might have said. He went on: 'I've got a story to tell you, *amigo*. It's kind of a confession, too, an' I don't want you to interrupt till I've finished it.'

'Go ahead, you old goat. I know you too well to be shocked at anything you may have done.'

It was a pretty commonplace sordid story but, as it went on, Lobo could understand why Jake (the old reprobate had always had a kind of integrity) had been reluctant to relive it, why in his half-crazy fever he had wanted to die rather than let his old friend Lobo learn of his shame. In the old days Lobo had been like a son to him.

When Jake first hit this territory he prospected up in the hills. But he never found anything and then one morning fell and broke his ankle. He began to crawl. He used up all his water and grub. He crawled miles under the blazing sun of the desert and rock out there. He found no more water. His ankle swelled like a balloon. By night he was delirious but in the morning he crawled again until he could crawl no more and lay there and shot off his last two bullets in what he thought a vain signal.

He was unconscious when Duke Roland, Clay Bogaine, Kid Moonlight and a few more of that band found him. They lit a fire, got him round and Duke Roland fixed up his ankle. By that night he was fairly fit again, and very grateful to his rescuers. It was then that Duke came forward with a proposition.

If Jake had turned down that proposition would they have let him live, he wondered? Or would he have been buried out there in the desert with a bullet in his brain to top off his busted ankle?

But that was no excuse. He was fed-up and he saw a chance to make some easy dinero and he took it. He was to be a look-out man for the gang, a contact man. Under his guise of an eccentric prospector he was to wander around the countryside and pick up information about rich ranch stock, shipments of money, bank set-ups and such like.

He made his sortie in Cravett from time to time. His Mad Jake role was a pose, of course, though he did admit that it seemed to come easily to him and he enjoyed shooting up the town. During his crazy merry-go-round he always managed to get what information he had gleaned to one of the band. He never took part in any of the raids — though that was no excuse either.

He finished. He made no excuse. But his old friend Lobo made excuses for him and they were genuine ones. Jake, the old soldier, was not the first man who had run with a wild bunch (and he hadn't actually done that!). Why, many of the most famous of the lawmen of the South-West had been owl-hooters in their days before they started to use their guns to support the law!

Lobo concluded, 'The information you have given me will help the law to wipe out this nest of sidewinders.'

He rose. 'I must go back to the jail and put this to old Mike. Hell, he won't judge you — he let things slide purty much himself an' he admits it.' He gripped Jake's shoulder. 'You get some sleep now, old-timer. We'll see you later.'

He was at the door when it burst open. Lopez cried, 'There's been some shooting down at the jail.'

Lobo ran through the mud and the rain, staggering, sloshing. He bumped into somebody in the darkness, recognized the irrascible tones of Doc Masters, made himself known to the little medico. They ran together, the plump little man puffing like a grampus, but finding enough breath to ask: 'What's goin' on at the jail? I heard somebody yell for me.'

'I dunno what's happened, but I'm scared for old Mike.'

He had reason to be — for the old

sheriff lay moaning in the open doorway of the cell-block. A couple of neighbours, drawn by the shooting, were bending over him. It was one of these who, seeing a light in the doctor's office just down the street, had yelled for him.

Masters took over. He could do more for Mike than any of them. There was only one thing Lobo could do. He ran past the group and into the passage. If that skunk had . . .

But Rabbit could not hurt anybody now. The cell was still locked and Rabbit lay on the floor in there, lay crumpled, strangely smaller now, in a pool of his own blood. He had been shot more than once in the chest and he was quite dead.

Lobo wondered whether Rabbit had got a gun from some place and shot it out with Mike. He couldn't see a gun in the cell. The keys were not anywhere around either. Lobo retraced his steps. Mike's gun and the keys were still in Mike's belt. Mike's breast was blood-stained, his shirt sopping with it. 'It's bad,' whispered Doc Masters. 'But I think he's got a chance.'

He moved aside a little and Lobo bent close to his old friend. He had a terrible feeling that he might have prevented this. He could have guarded against it. If he had spoken, Lopez would have come and stayed with Mike while Lobo was with Jake Morgan.

Mike seemed to sense the gaze of those eyes and he opened his own eyes.

'Lobo,' he croaked.

His eyes implored. Lobo bent closer. Mike's lips framed another name.

'Duke Roland.'

Then his eyes closed again.

'He's unconscious,' said the doctor. 'I think it's safe to move him now. Help me get him on to the couch.'

Lobo obeyed mechanically, helping the little medico and the other two men carry the unconscious bulk of the sheriff to the couch in the office. Then Lobo, almost like a man in a dream, his eyes cold, horrible, moved apart from the others and checked his gun, his cartridges.

His eyes rested for a moment on the star which lay on the desk, gleaming a little beneath the light. His star. But he did not pick it up and put it on.

He left the office. He did not seem to see the people who clustered outside, did not seem to hear their questions.

Duke Roland sat in his luxurious little cabin on the edge of the town. He was in trousers and vest. The light gleamed on his thick raven hair, his high cheekbones, the pure silk of his shirt. He was a fine figure of a man. The couch on which he sat was decorated by a beautiful Indian blanket. On this lay Duke's gunbelt, a beautiful arrangement of polished embossed leather, chased with silver. Duke was cleaning his guns, fondling them lovingly with his long, white, well-tended, gambler's hands, gunfighter's hands.

There was a knock on the door.

Duke spun the cylinder of the gun he held, pointed it at the door, called 'Come in'.

The door opened. Duke lowered the gun.

The visitor was one of his men. One of the lesser jackals. A little man with a white face shaped like a triangle, set off by batlike ears. His appearance was totally unprepossessing. He was insignificant, not worthy of a part in any story concerning men. But, because nobody took much notice of him, he was valuable as a picker-up of information, a gleaner of trifles seemingly as insignificant as himself, but which might be used by a lawless organization.

But the item of news he had brought tonight was far from significant and he blurted it out excitedly.

'Boss, Lobo Watkins is out in town huntin' for you. Mike Daventry ain't dead.'

Duke lost his sang-froid. 'The old buzzard must be made of iron. I was sure . . . '

He broke off. This was a setback he hadn't bargained for: that Mike would live to name his would-be murderer and the murderer of Rabbit, another man who might have talked. But Duke's mind was already working fast and after a moment he said: 'Listen to me now. Listen carefully.'

'Sure, boss.'

'I'm leaving this place. It doesn't suit me to meet Lobo Watkins right now. I'll take care of him in my own good time . . .'

'Sure you will, boss.'

'Listen!' he said. 'I'll be back in the morning. I want you to go around town and pass the word to the boys. Tell them to get ready for a big job. Be very careful — if you give the game away to anybody else I'll tear your guts out . . .'

'You can count on me, boss.'

'All right! Then at dawn I want you to meet me down at the cottonwoods by the creek. Get that!'

'I got that, boss. Dawn. Dawn at the cottonwoods by the creek. Sure, boss.'

'Get goin', then.'

The little man with the triangular white face and the bat ears took his leave. Duke Roland prepared to leave his cosy billet for a few hours. But he had another billet and a certain young lady who would keep him company there. He smiled mockingly: the quixotic Lobo would certainly not look for him in a lady's boudoir.

★   ★   ★

At the grey of dawn Lobo Watkins was sitting in the swivel-chair in the sheriff's office with his feet up on the desk. He dozed fitfully. He had been out half the night and had arrived back sodden and wretched without even getting a smell of his quarry.

Mike lay on the couch with Doc Masters beside him. Mike was still unconscious, breathing shallowly. The Doc had told Lobo to go to bed, but the stubborn man would not: he dozed at the desk, he aimed to go out again.

He was thinking that Mad Jake Morgan's indictment of Duke Roland had come a little too late. An ironical twist. Duke had overplayed his hand, indicted himself. But that would be little consolation if Mike died and all Lobo could do was try and fix it so that Duke cashed in his chips too. Lobo was banking on the fact that Duke had too much pride to run away with his tail between his legs.

It was still raining. Main street was a river of mud. For days wagons had not been able to negotiate it and people kept to the sidewalks as much as possible. Even the duckboard bridges were beginning to sink beneath the ooze.

The skies got slowly lighter, an unreal metallic light. Heels tapped sharply on the sidewalk and the door was flung open.

Once more it was little brown-eyed Manuel, sidekick of Lopez of the livery. He was mud-bespattered, breathing hard.

'Señor Lobo,' he shrilled. 'Duke Roland is in the street by Mees Sadie's place. He ees waitin' for you.'

'Come in, son,' said Lobo gently.

He rose and buckled on his gunbelt and checked his gun and cartridges.

Doc Masters said: 'Watch out for tricks, Lobo.'

'Sure, Doc.'

But Lobo, understanding the overweening vanity of a man like Duke, did not think there would be any tricks. Duke was a gambler and a gunfighter. Duke thought he could never lose. In fact, he probably figured that with this bold grandstand play he still stood a good chance of winning all along the line.

Lobo put on his hat and his leather vest. He squeezed the boy's shoulder. 'Stay here, *amigo*.'

'Yes, *amigo*.' The boy showed a flash of white teeth. Then as Lobo reached the door the boy cried, 'Señor Lobo, you will beat the peeg. You will beat him, *amigo*.'

With the childish treble ringing in his ears, Lobo closed the door behind him and began to walk.

The street was empty, as well it might be. Lobo kept to the boardwalk. The mud lapped at its edges. At first he could not see Duke. Then, as he got nearer to Sadie's place, Duke stepped off the sidewalk and on to one of the duckboards and strode into the centre of the street. Lobo, too, chose one of the firmer-looking duckboards, and followed suit. They faced each other, good shooting distance between them, and a black oily morass.

Neither of them spoke.

Lobo was bent a little. He seemed to be lounging. Duke, mindful of the faces at the windows all along the street, stood more erect. He was faultlessly dressed, his broadcloth swept back to reveal the pearl handles of his guns.

His shoulders shrugged, he dropped his hands.

Lobo Watkins's right shoulder dipped as if he had suddenly got a little more tired on that side.

Nobody could have watched both men. Their movements were a blur. But everybody heard the two shots and many realized that they had both come from the same gun.

Duke Roland teetered on his duckboard, his hands clawing at his breast. His guns had already been swallowed up by the black slime at his feet. His beautiful pearl-grey sombrero had fallen off and it floated there. Duke's black hair had broken apart in disarray. Lobo stood with his smoking gun hanging laxly at the end of one lean arm, and he watched.

Duke Roland pitched forward into the mud. The viscid black stuff sucked hungrily at the dead face.

A little man with a triangular white face and bat ears ran from Sadie's place. He screamed something and raised a gun and fired at Lobo.

By a strange fluke of chance — for no man could be that good a shot with such split-second timing — the slug hit

Lobo's gun and knocked it from his hand. The mud swallowed it, chuckling.

Another shot rang out from Sadie's place. The little man — an unknown factor, now forever unknown — had reached his horse; but he fell there, a bullet in the back of his head.

Gun in hand, Bruno Jensen came out on to the sidewalk.

'Hey, boss,' he called. 'You dropped your gun!'

Lobo took his gaze away from the bodies in the mud. He bent and retrieved his gun, held it gingerly. He negotiated the sidewalk and strolled towards Bruno. The brooding look went from his face; he even smiled a little.

'Who's been teaching you to shoot?' he said.

* * *

The Craddock — Cravett feud had begun with a bloody battle, following the lynching of Cal Jensen, culminating in the death of King Craddock. The

253

feud finished with a battle: mercifully a comparatively bloodless one. Sadie Cane, who trusted her friend George Pinfold far more than the law did, had sent a message to the Craddock ranch. And, as if the shooting of Duke Roland and his insignificant minion had been a signal, the Craddock men rode into town at the crucial moment.

They split into two parties, one led by George Pinfold, the other by moonfaced Brinny Capes. The Roland boys, demoralised by the death of their leader, were driven like sheep. They grabbed what they could, and ran for their horses. Many were caught and roughly handled, dipped in the horse-troughs, dragged in the mud, before being sped on their way by some fancy shooting.

Duke Roland had planned to kill Lobo Watkins and then lead his men on a wholesale raid on the Craddock ranch. He had figured on taking over Cravett territory for once and for all.

Now he lay with his handsome face

in the mud, trampled on, forgotten.

And the day came to an end.

A few more days passed before the Lobo Watkins faction left town. Lobo, Bruno and Jake Morgan rode ahead of the noonday stage. Jake, who had been a cowhand in his younger days, aimed to be one again. He desired no better boss than his old sidekick, El Lobo.

In the coach behind them rode Lucinda Sanders and Sadie Cane. Sadie had sold all her holdings in Cravett to Mr Rafe Spalletti, the Chicago businessman. She said she didn't aim to let Lobo get away from her this time. But she didn't need to chase him after all. In fact he kept galloping his horse back to the coach, in case Sadie had changed her mind and he'd have to hog-tie her or some thing.

Sheriff Mike Daventry was mending quickly. He was going to be all right. He aimed to visit the Watkins' spread in good time for the double wedding that was due to take place in a week or so.

BRAZOS STATION

Clayton Nash

Caleb Brett liked his job as deputy sheriff and being betrothed to the sheriff's daughter, Rose. What he didn't like was the thought of the sheriff moving in with them once they were married. But capturing the infamous outlaw Gil Bannerman offered a way out because there was plenty of reward money. Then came Brett's big mistake — he lost Bannerman and was framed. Now everything he treasured was lost. Did he have a chance in hell of fighting his way back?

DEAD IS FOR EVER

Amy Sadler

After rescuing Hope Bennett from the clutches of two trailbums, Sam Carver made a serious mistake. He killed one of the outlaws, and reckoned on collecting the bounty on Lew Daggett. But catching Sam off-guard, Daggett made off with the girl, leaving Sam for dead. However, he was only grazed and once he came to, he set out in search of Hope. When he eventually found her, he was forced into a dramatic showdown with his life on the line.